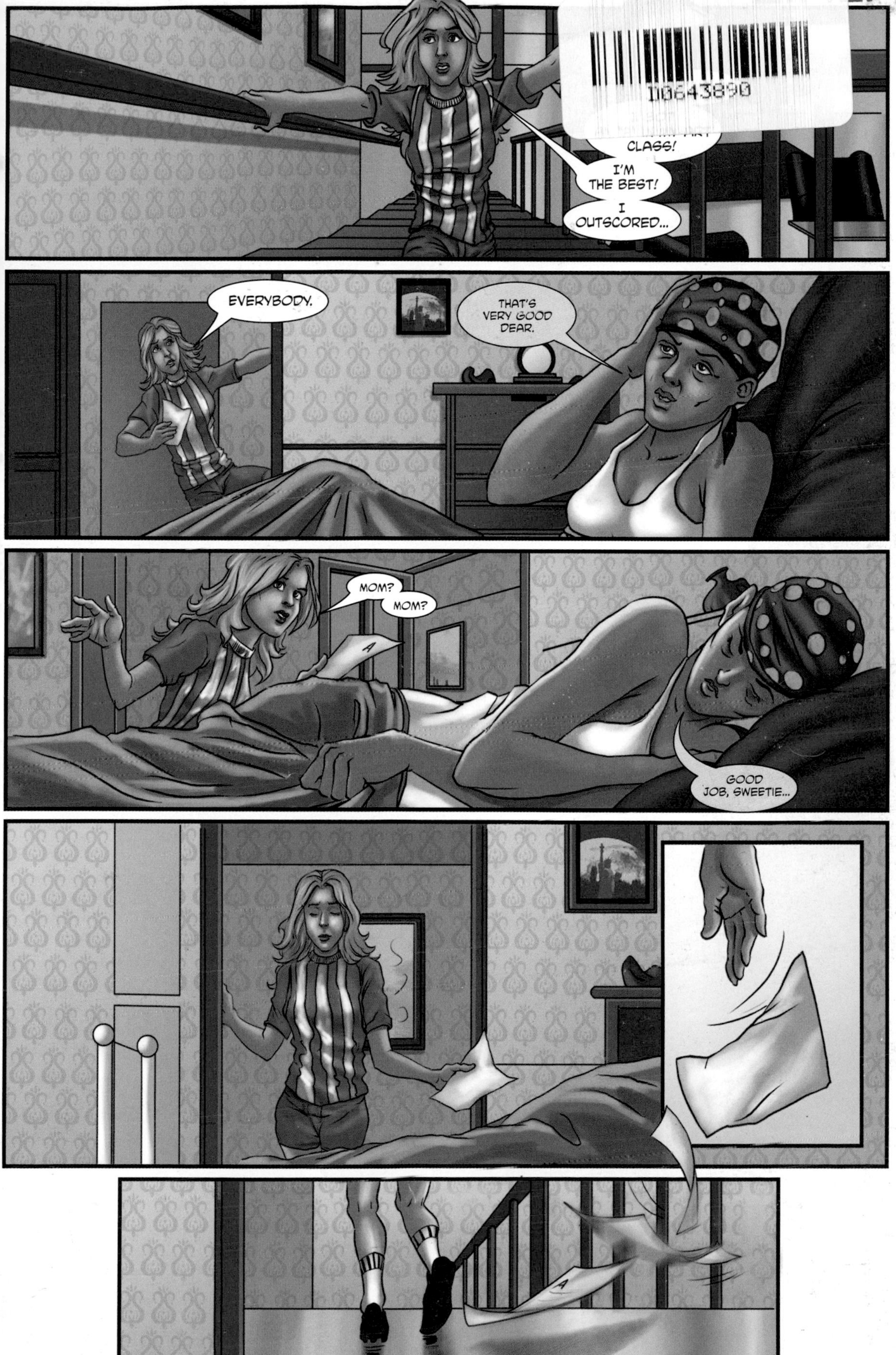
CLASS!
I'M THE BEST!
I OUTSCORED...
EVERYBODY.
THAT'S VERY GOOD DEAR.
MOM?
MOM?
GOOD JOB, SWEETIE...

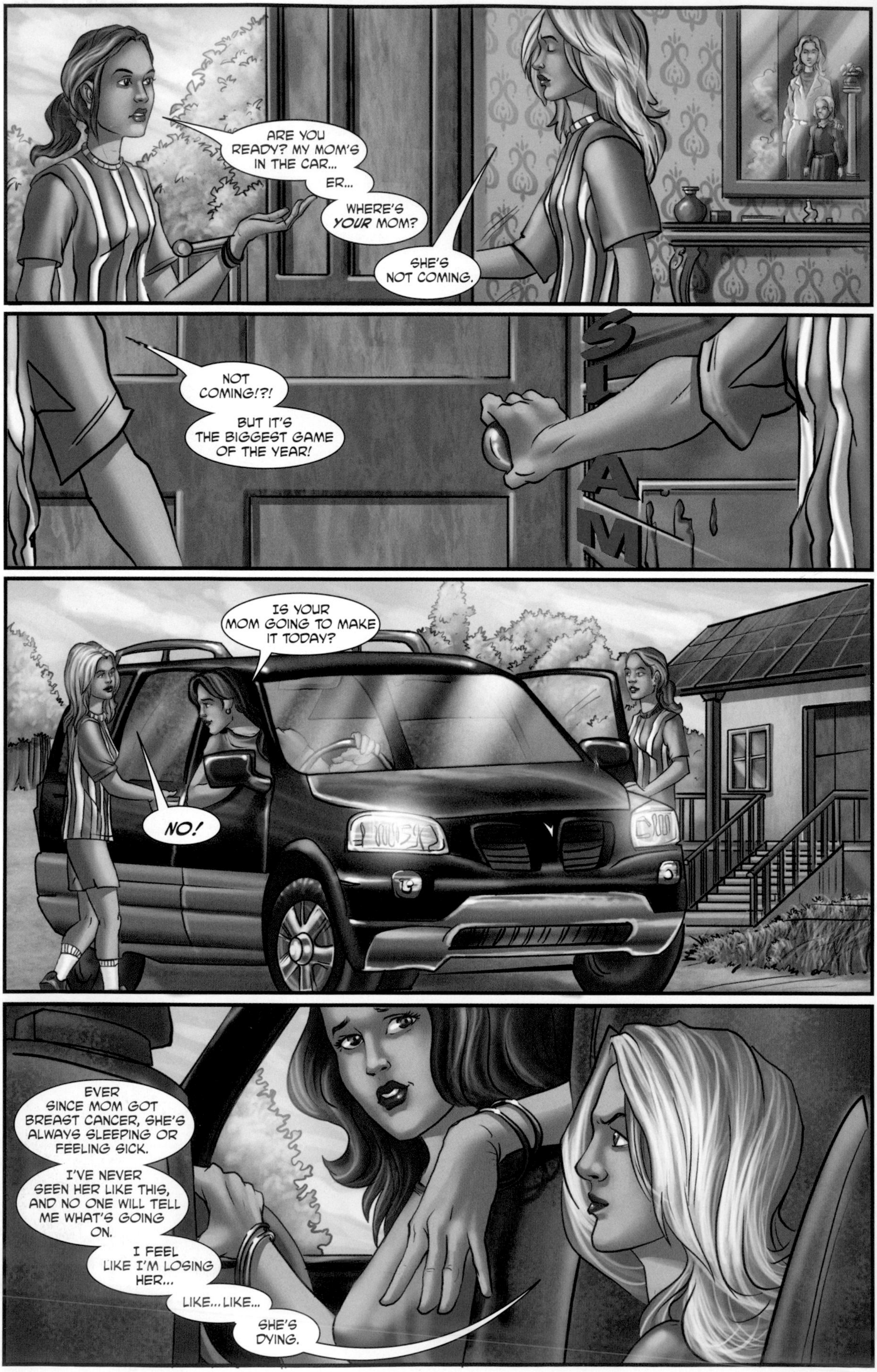
ARE YOU READY? MY MOM'S IN THE CAR...
ER...
WHERE'S *YOUR* MOM?
SHE'S NOT COMING.
S L A M
NOT COMING!?!
BUT IT'S THE BIGGEST GAME OF THE YEAR!
IS YOUR MOM GOING TO MAKE IT TODAY?
NO!
EVER SINCE MOM GOT BREAST CANCER, SHE'S ALWAYS SLEEPING OR FEELING SICK.
I'VE NEVER SEEN HER LIKE THIS, AND NO ONE WILL TELL ME WHAT'S GOING ON.
I FEEL LIKE I'M LOSING HER...
LIKE... LIKE...
SHE'S DYING.

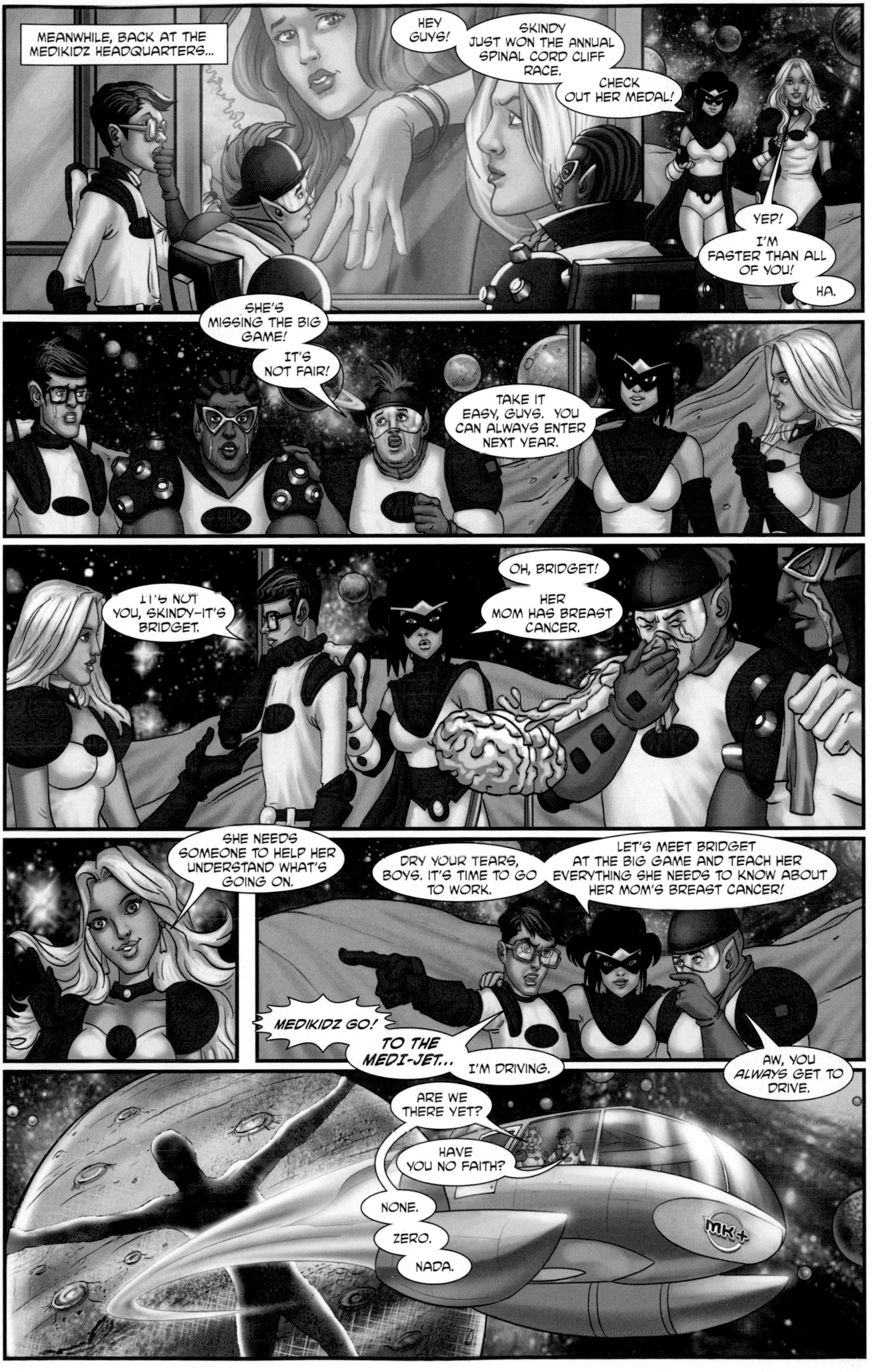
MEANWHILE, BACK AT THE MEDIKIDZ HEADQUARTERS...
HEY GUYS!
SKINDY JUST WON THE ANNUAL SPINAL CORD CLIFF RACE.
CHECK OUT HER MEDAL!
YEP!
I'M FASTER THAN ALL OF YOU!
HA.
SHE'S MISSING THE BIG GAME!
IT'S NOT FAIR!
TAKE IT EASY, GUYS. YOU CAN ALWAYS ENTER NEXT YEAR.
IT'S NOT YOU, SKINDY–IT'S BRIDGET.
OH, BRIDGET!
HER MOM HAS BREAST CANCER.
SHE NEEDS SOMEONE TO HELP HER UNDERSTAND WHAT'S GOING ON.
DRY YOUR TEARS, BOYS. IT'S TIME TO GO TO WORK.
LET'S MEET BRIDGET AT THE BIG GAME AND TEACH HER EVERYTHING SHE NEEDS TO KNOW ABOUT HER MOM'S BREAST CANCER!
MEDIKIDZ GO!
TO THE MEDI-JET...
I'M DRIVING.
AW, YOU ALWAYS GET TO DRIVE.
ARE WE THERE YET?
HAVE YOU NO FAITH?
NONE.
ZERO.
NADA.
MK+

SEE? I TOLD YOU! ANOTHER PERFECT...

LANDING.

OOOOoooooOOOoooooo.

CRASH!!!

WHACK!

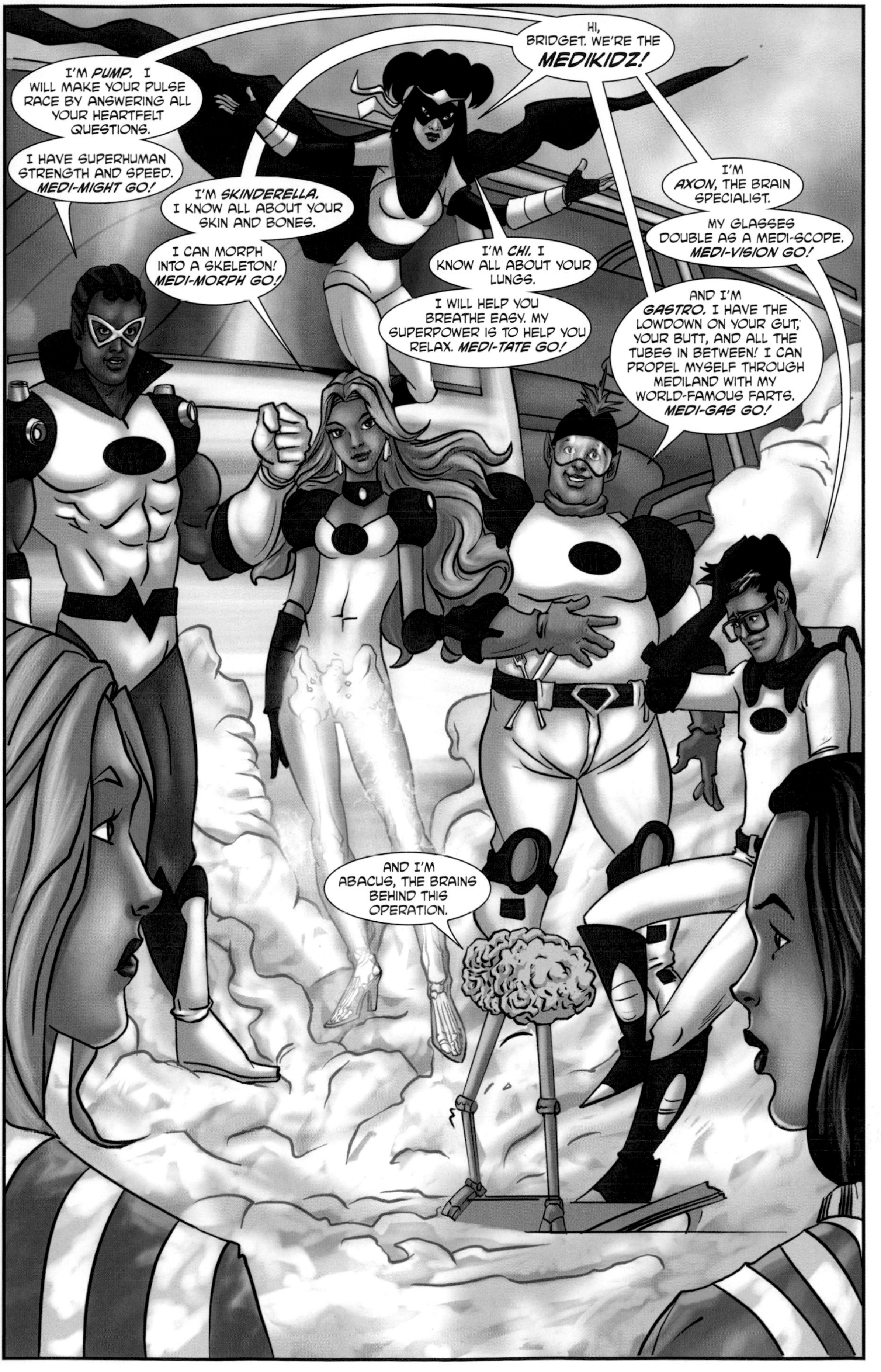
HI, BRIDGET. WE'RE THE MEDIKIDZ!
I'M PUMP. I WILL MAKE YOUR PULSE RACE BY ANSWERING ALL YOUR HEARTFELT QUESTIONS.
I HAVE SUPERHUMAN STRENGTH AND SPEED. MEDI-MIGHT GO!
I'M SKINDERELLA. I KNOW ALL ABOUT YOUR SKIN AND BONES.
I CAN MORPH INTO A SKELETON! MEDI-MORPH GO!
I'M CHI. I KNOW ALL ABOUT YOUR LUNGS.
I WILL HELP YOU BREATHE EASY. MY SUPERPOWER IS TO HELP YOU RELAX. MEDI-TATE GO!
I'M AXON, THE BRAIN SPECIALIST.
MY GLASSES DOUBLE AS A MEDI-SCOPE. MEDI-VISION GO!
AND I'M GASTRO. I HAVE THE LOWDOWN ON YOUR GUT, YOUR BUTT, AND ALL THE TUBES IN BETWEEN! I CAN PROPEL MYSELF THROUGH MEDILAND WITH MY WORLD-FAMOUS FARTS. MEDI-GAS GO!
AND I'M ABACUS, THE BRAINS BEHIND THIS OPERATION.

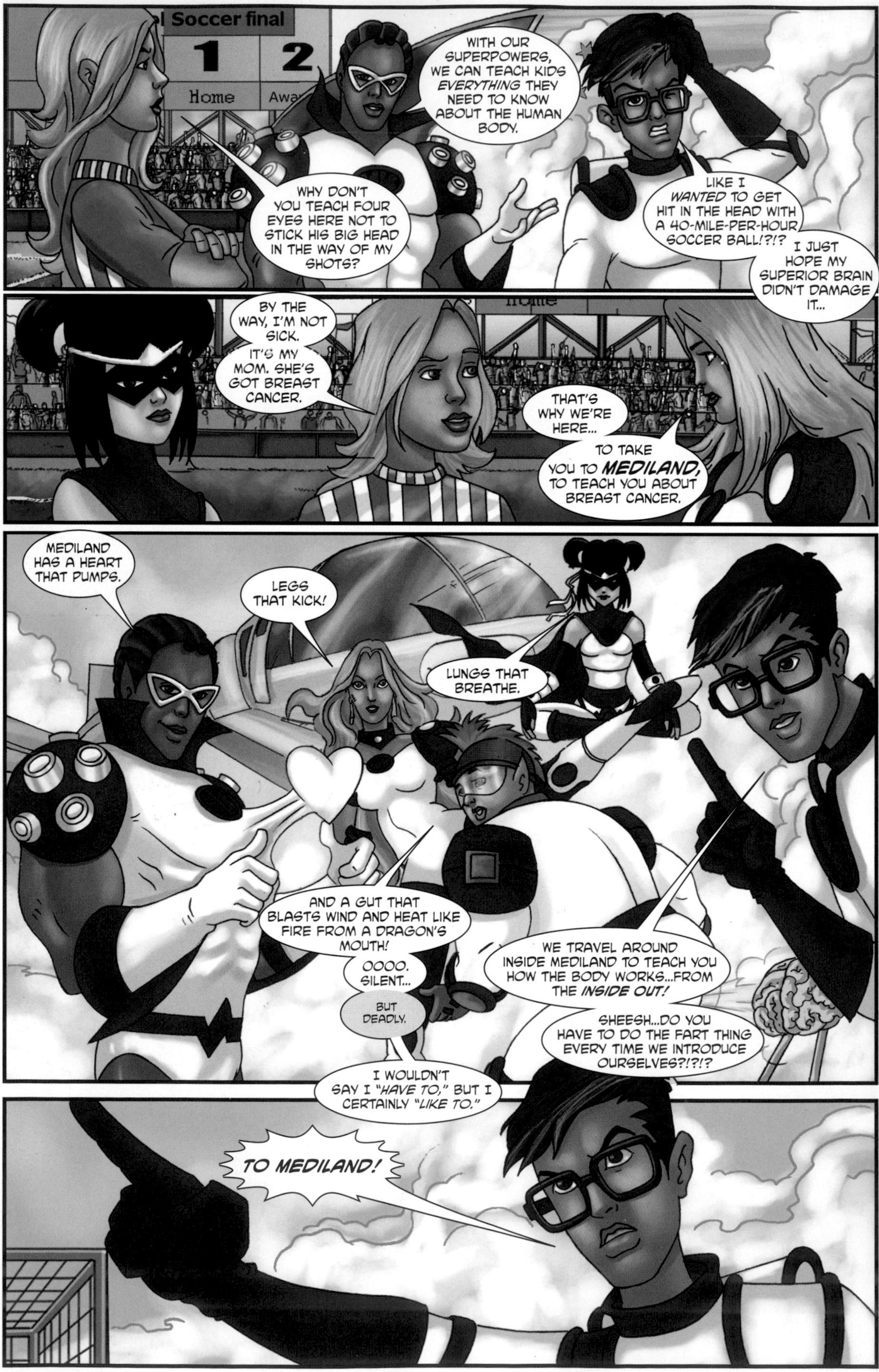
Soccer final
1 2
Home Away
WITH OUR SUPERPOWERS, WE CAN TEACH KIDS *EVERYTHING* THEY NEED TO KNOW ABOUT THE HUMAN BODY.
WHY DON'T YOU TEACH FOUR EYES HERE NOT TO STICK HIS BIG HEAD IN THE WAY OF MY SHOTS?
LIKE I *WANTED* TO GET HIT IN THE HEAD WITH A 40-MILE-PER-HOUR SOCCER BALL!?!?
I JUST HOPE MY SUPERIOR BRAIN DIDN'T DAMAGE IT...
BY THE WAY, I'M NOT SICK.
IT'S MY MOM. SHE'S GOT BREAST CANCER.
THAT'S WHY WE'RE HERE...
TO TAKE YOU TO ***MEDILAND,*** TO TEACH YOU ABOUT BREAST CANCER.
MEDILAND HAS A HEART THAT PUMPS.
LEGS THAT KICK!
LUNGS THAT BREATHE.
AND A GUT THAT BLASTS WIND AND HEAT LIKE FIRE FROM A DRAGON'S MOUTH!
OOOO. SILENT...
BUT DEADLY.
WE TRAVEL AROUND INSIDE MEDILAND TO TEACH YOU HOW THE BODY WORKS...FROM THE *INSIDE OUT!*
SHEESH...DO YOU HAVE TO DO THE FART THING EVERY TIME WE INTRODUCE OURSELVES?!?!?
I WOULDN'T SAY I "*HAVE TO,*" BUT I CERTAINLY "*LIKE TO.*"
TO MEDILAND!

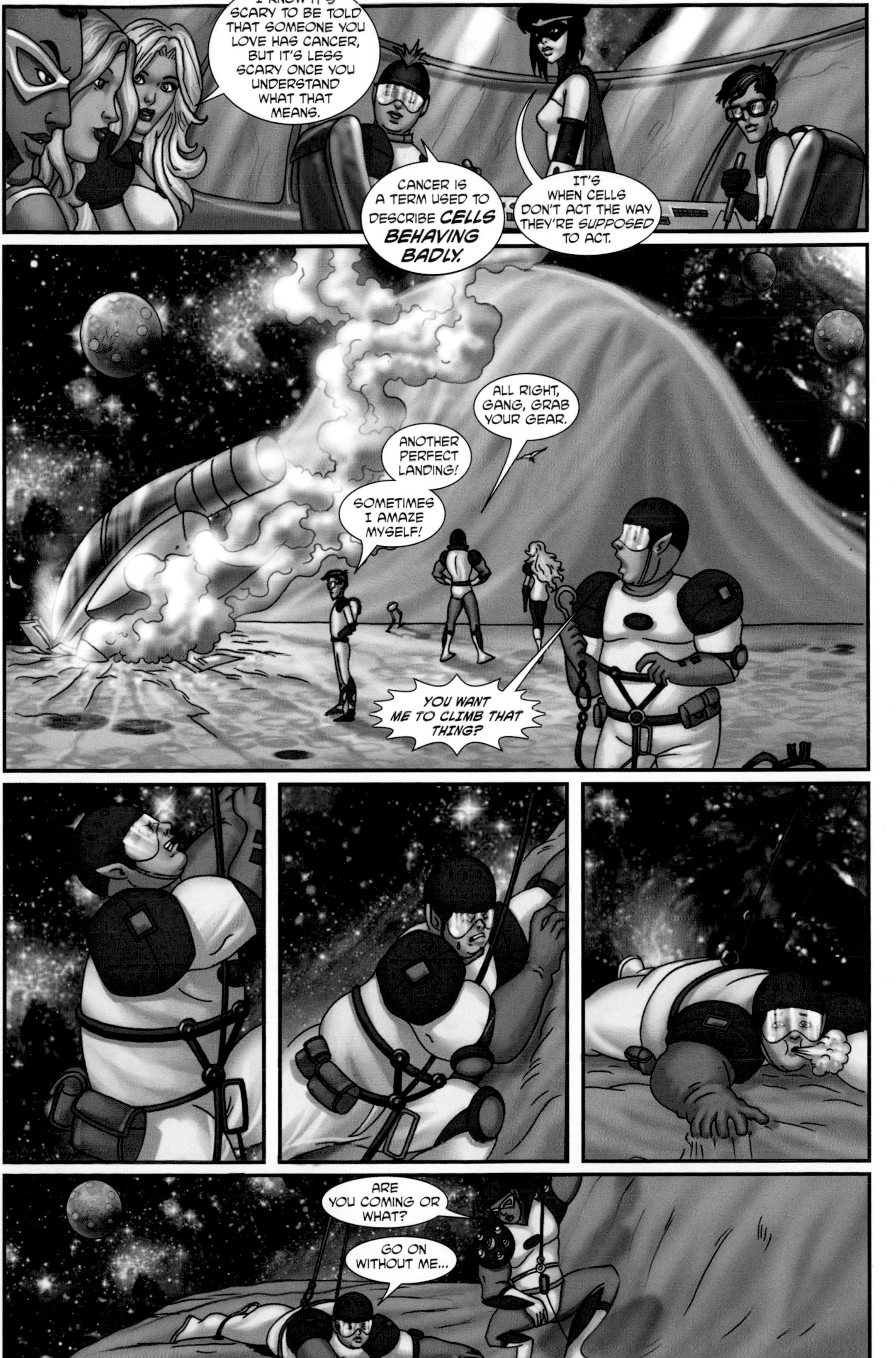
I KNOW IT'S SCARY TO BE TOLD THAT SOMEONE YOU LOVE HAS CANCER, BUT IT'S LESS SCARY ONCE YOU UNDERSTAND WHAT THAT MEANS.
CANCER IS A TERM USED TO DESCRIBE CELLS BEHAVING BADLY.
IT'S WHEN CELLS DON'T ACT THE WAY THEY'RE SUPPOSED TO ACT.
ALL RIGHT, GANG, GRAB YOUR GEAR.
ANOTHER PERFECT LANDING!
SOMETIMES I AMAZE MYSELF!
YOU WANT ME TO CLIMB THAT THING?
ARE YOU COMING OR WHAT?
GO ON WITHOUT ME...

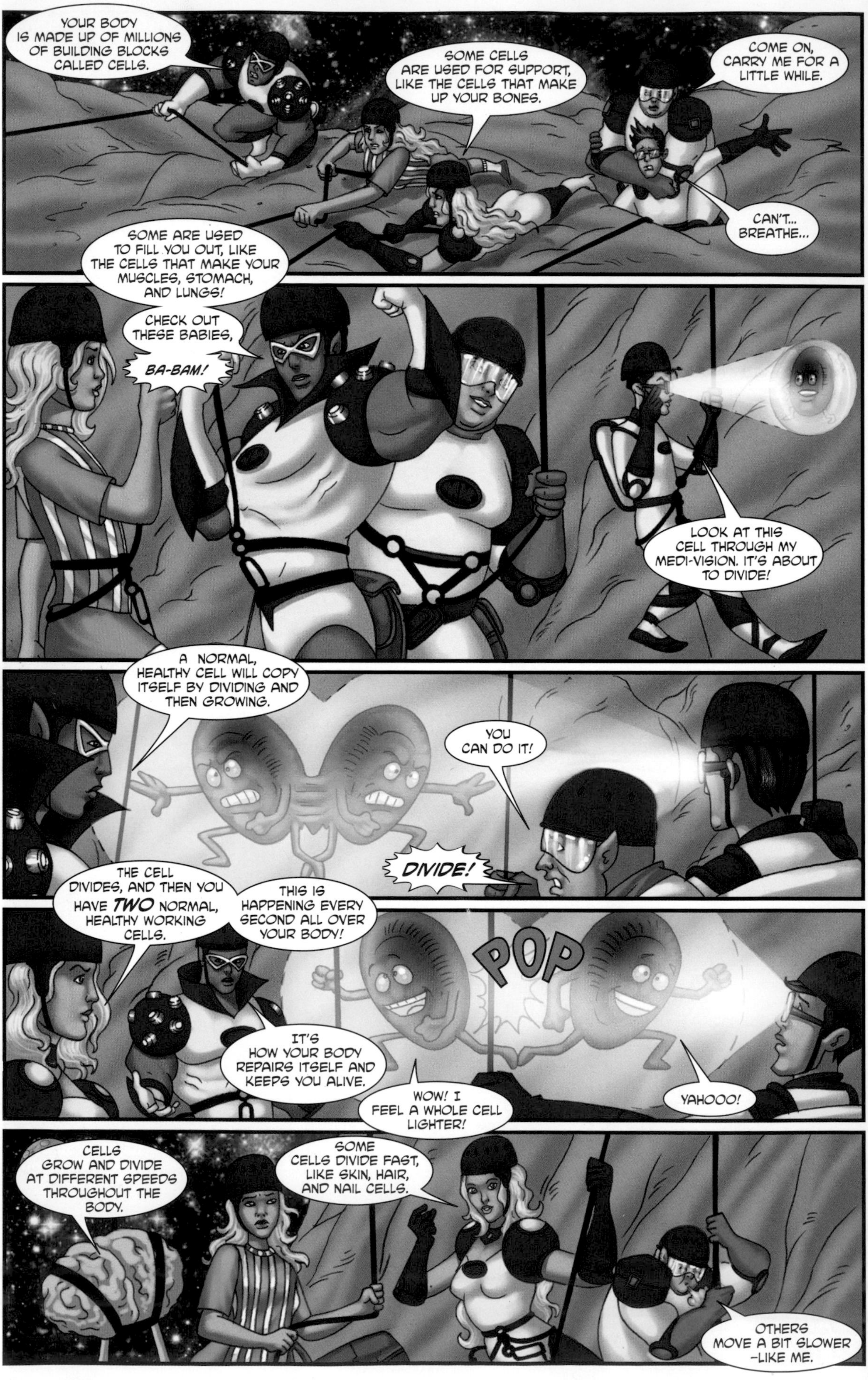
YOUR BODY IS MADE UP OF MILLIONS OF BUILDING BLOCKS CALLED CELLS.
SOME CELLS ARE USED FOR SUPPORT, LIKE THE CELLS THAT MAKE UP YOUR BONES.
COME ON, CARRY ME FOR A LITTLE WHILE.
CAN'T... BREATHE...
SOME ARE USED TO FILL YOU OUT, LIKE THE CELLS THAT MAKE YOUR MUSCLES, STOMACH, AND LUNGS!
CHECK OUT THESE BABIES,
BA-BAM!
LOOK AT THIS CELL THROUGH MY MEDI-VISION. IT'S ABOUT TO DIVIDE!
A NORMAL, HEALTHY CELL WILL COPY ITSELF BY DIVIDING AND THEN GROWING.
YOU CAN DO IT!
DIVIDE!
THE CELL DIVIDES, AND THEN YOU HAVE **TWO** NORMAL, HEALTHY WORKING CELLS.
THIS IS HAPPENING EVERY SECOND ALL OVER YOUR BODY!
POP
IT'S HOW YOUR BODY REPAIRS ITSELF AND KEEPS YOU ALIVE.
WOW! I FEEL A WHOLE CELL LIGHTER!
YAHOOO!
CELLS GROW AND DIVIDE AT DIFFERENT SPEEDS THROUGHOUT THE BODY.
SOME CELLS DIVIDE FAST, LIKE SKIN, HAIR, AND NAIL CELLS.
OTHERS MOVE A BIT SLOWER –LIKE ME.

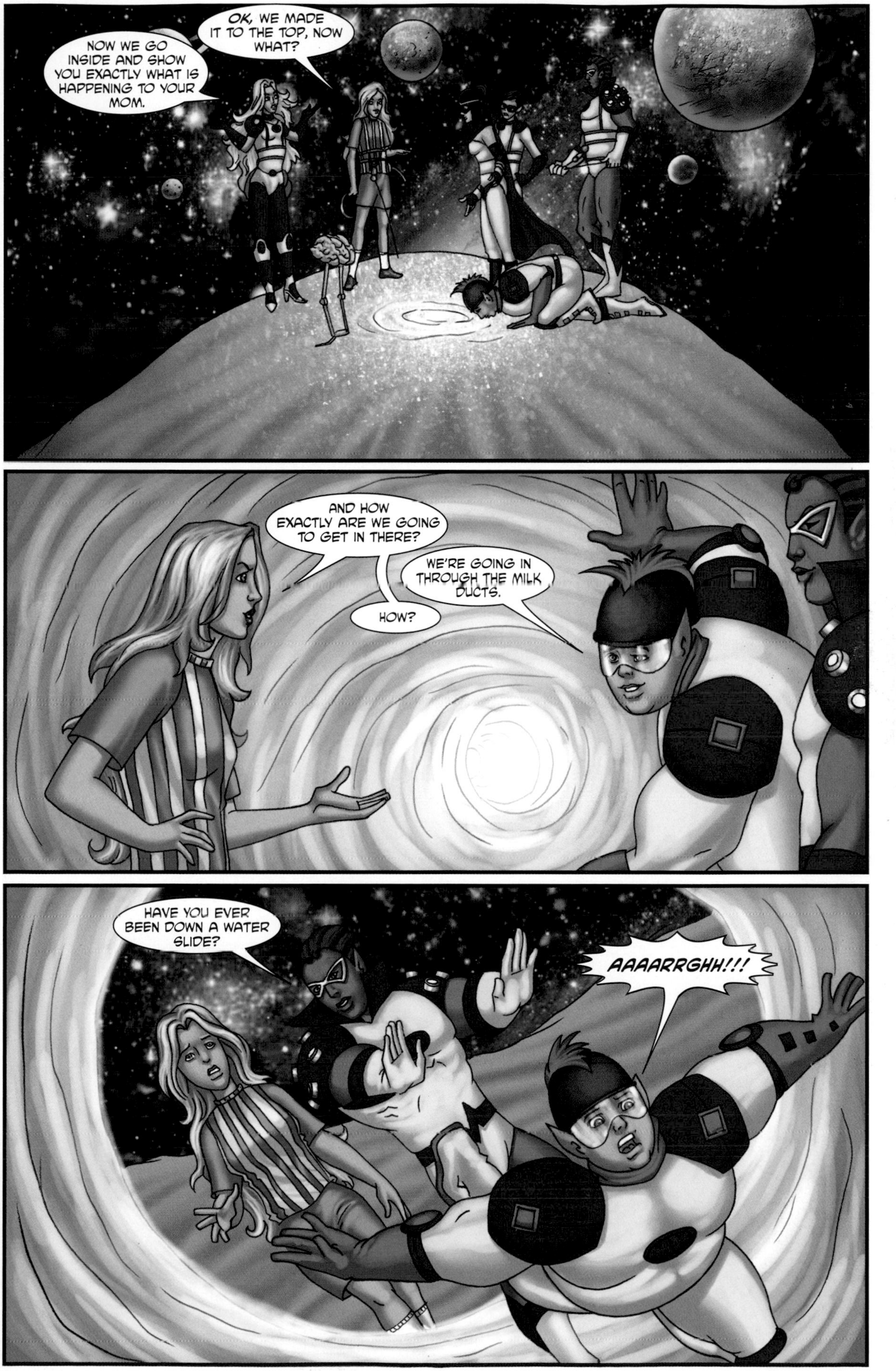
NOW WE GO INSIDE AND SHOW YOU EXACTLY WHAT IS HAPPENING TO YOUR MOM.
OK, WE MADE IT TO THE TOP, NOW WHAT?
AND HOW EXACTLY ARE WE GOING TO GET IN THERE?
WE'RE GOING IN THROUGH THE MILK DUCTS.
HOW?
HAVE YOU EVER BEEN DOWN A WATER SLIDE?
AAAARRGHH!!!

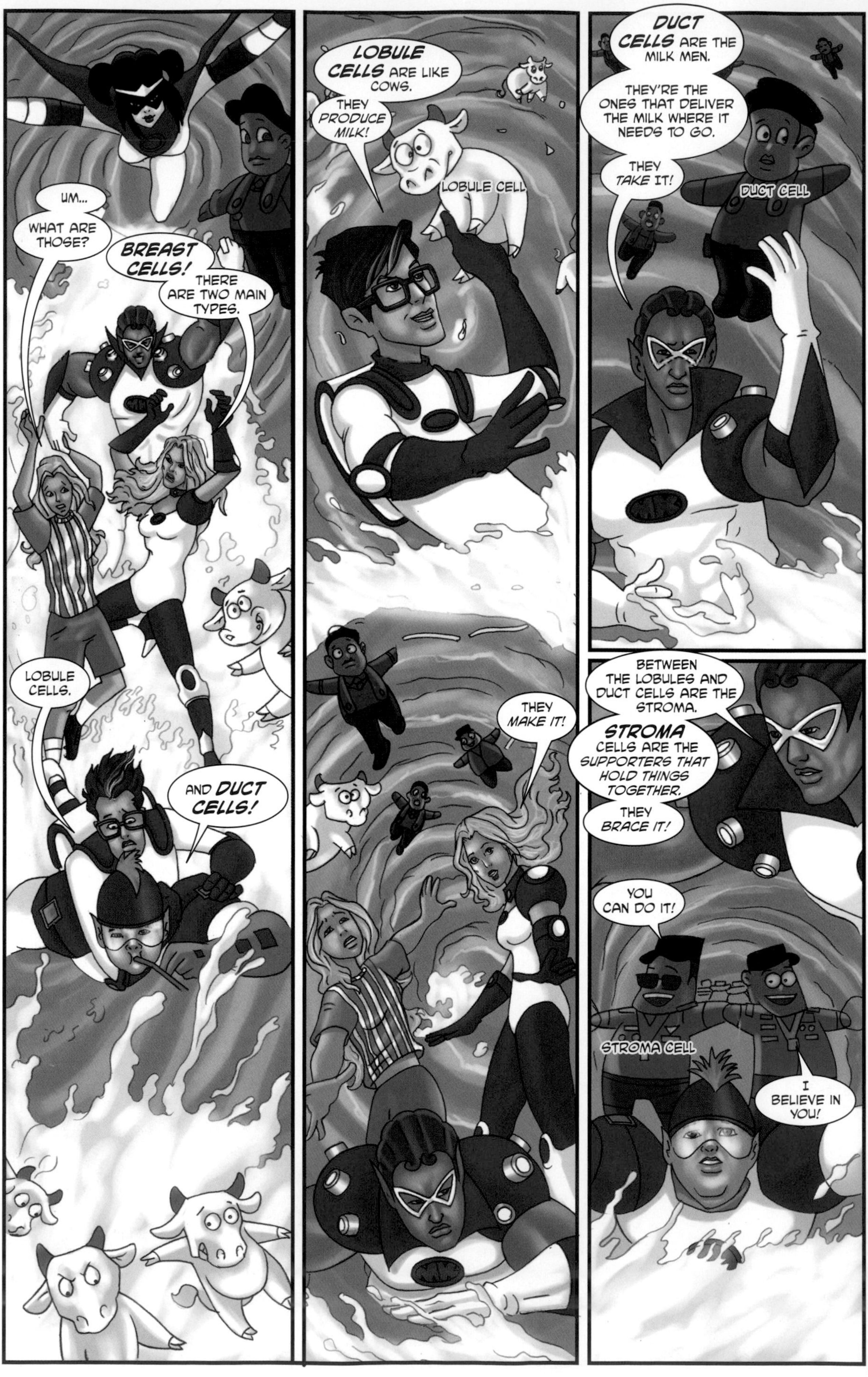
UM...
WHAT ARE THOSE?
BREAST CELLS!
THERE ARE TWO MAIN TYPES.
LOBULE CELLS.
AND DUCT CELLS!
LOBULE CELLS ARE LIKE COWS.
THEY PRODUCE MILK!
LOBULE CELL
THEY MAKE IT!
DUCT CELLS ARE THE MILK MEN.
THEY'RE THE ONES THAT DELIVER THE MILK WHERE IT NEEDS TO GO.
THEY TAKE IT!
DUCT CELL
BETWEEN THE LOBULES AND DUCT CELLS ARE THE STROMA.
STROMA CELLS ARE THE SUPPORTERS THAT HOLD THINGS TOGETHER.
THEY BRACE IT!
YOU CAN DO IT!
STROMA CELL
I BELIEVE IN YOU!

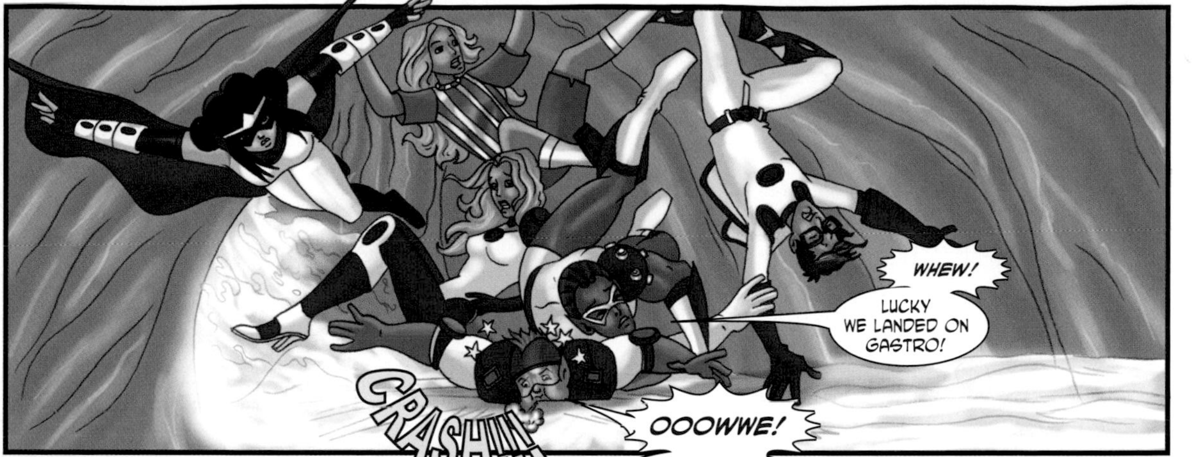
WHEW!
LUCKY WE LANDED ON GASTRO!
CRASH!!!!
OOOWWE!

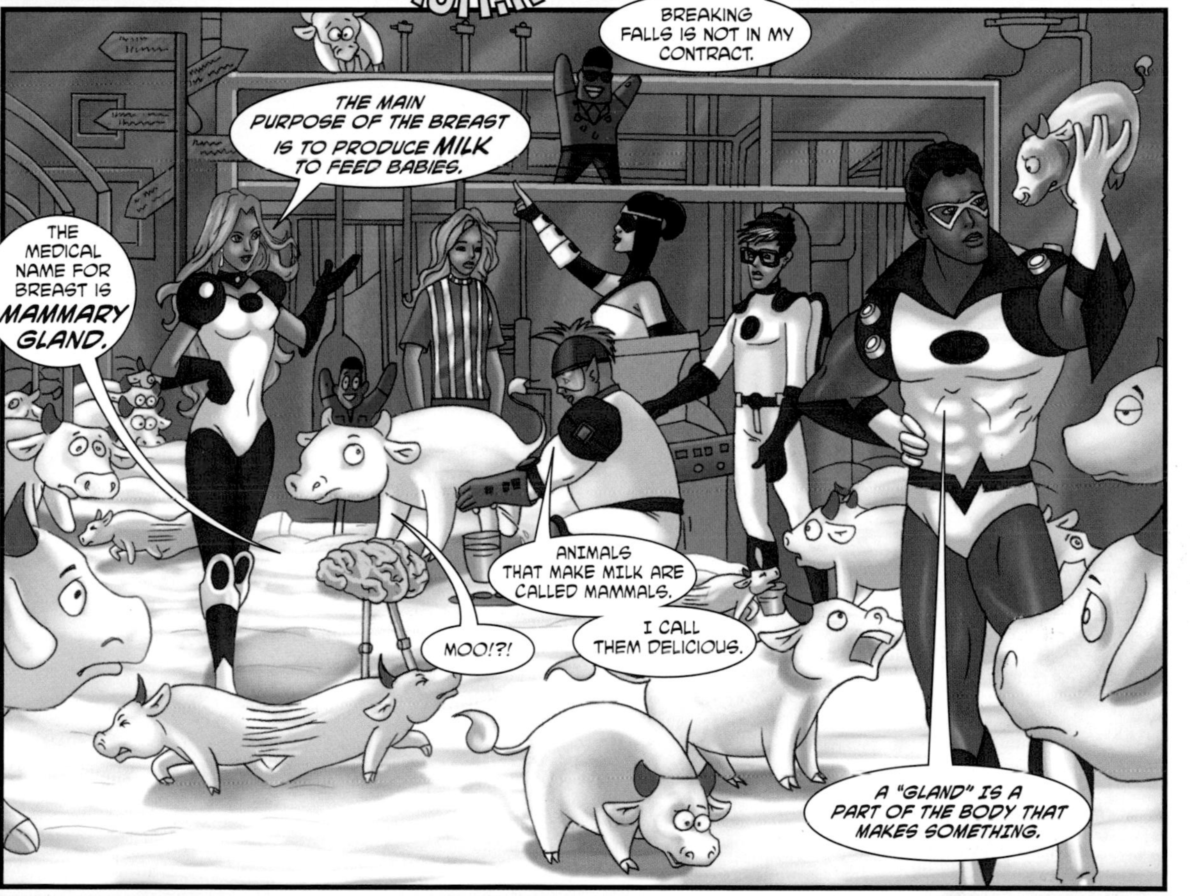
BREAKING FALLS IS NOT IN MY CONTRACT.
THE MAIN PURPOSE OF THE BREAST IS TO PRODUCE MILK TO FEED BABIES.
THE MEDICAL NAME FOR BREAST IS MAMMARY GLAND.
ANIMALS THAT MAKE MILK ARE CALLED MAMMALS.
MOO!?!
I CALL THEM DELICIOUS.
A "GLAND" IS A PART OF THE BODY THAT MAKES SOMETHING.

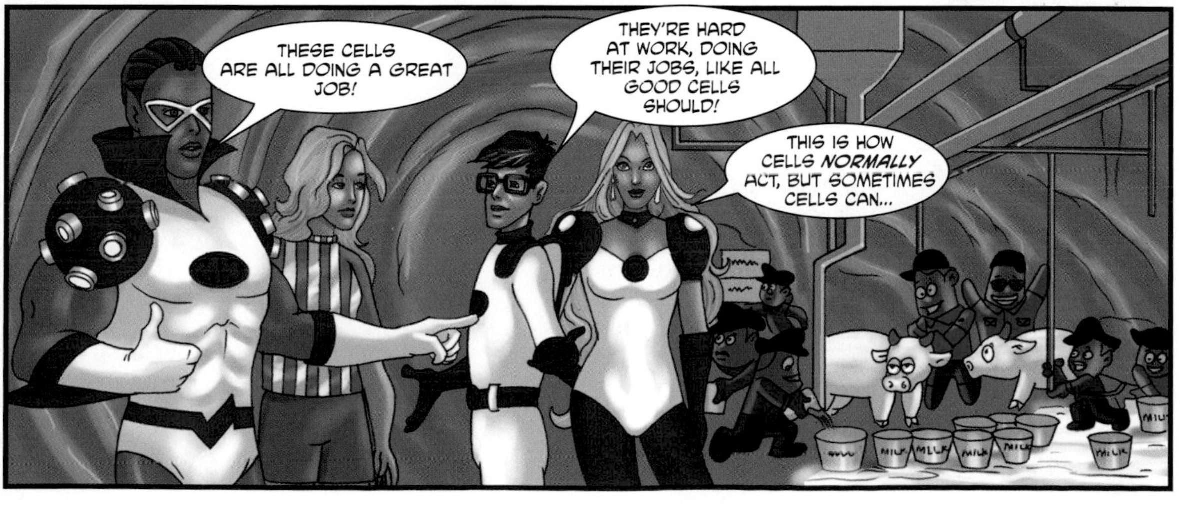
THESE CELLS ARE ALL DOING A GREAT JOB!
THEY'RE HARD AT WORK, DOING THEIR JOBS, LIKE ALL GOOD CELLS SHOULD!
THIS IS HOW CELLS NORMALLY ACT, BUT SOMETIMES CELLS CAN...

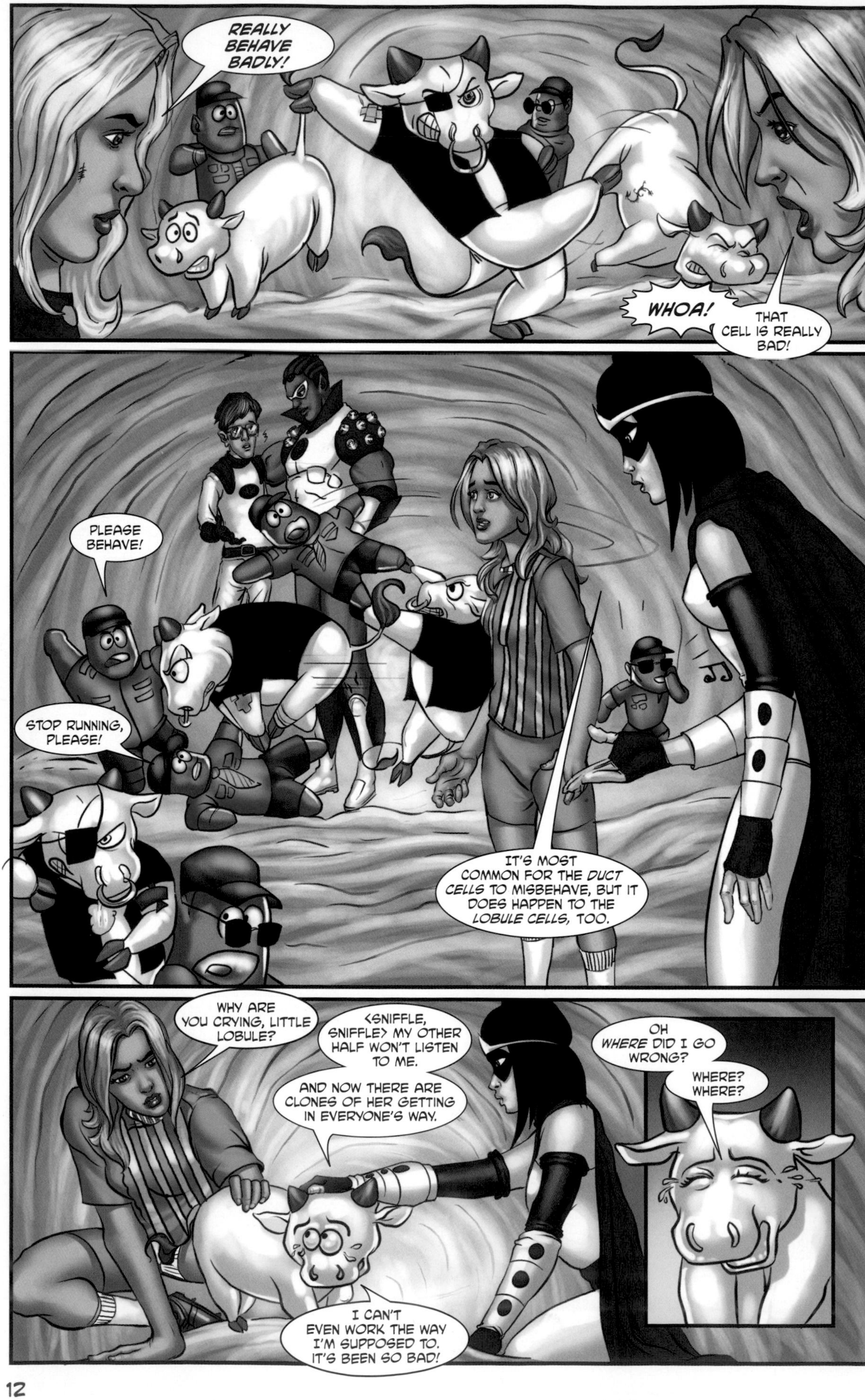
REALLY BEHAVE BADLY!
WHOA!
THAT CELL IS REALLY BAD!
PLEASE BEHAVE!
STOP RUNNING, PLEASE!
IT'S MOST COMMON FOR THE *DUCT CELLS* TO MISBEHAVE, BUT IT DOES HAPPEN TO THE *LOBULE CELLS,* TOO.
WHY ARE YOU CRYING, LITTLE LOBULE?
<SNIFFLE, SNIFFLE> MY OTHER HALF WON'T LISTEN TO ME.
AND NOW THERE ARE CLONES OF HER GETTING IN EVERYONE'S WAY.
I CAN'T EVEN WORK THE WAY I'M SUPPOSED TO. IT'S BEEN SO BAD!
OH *WHERE* DID I GO WRONG?
WHERE? WHERE?

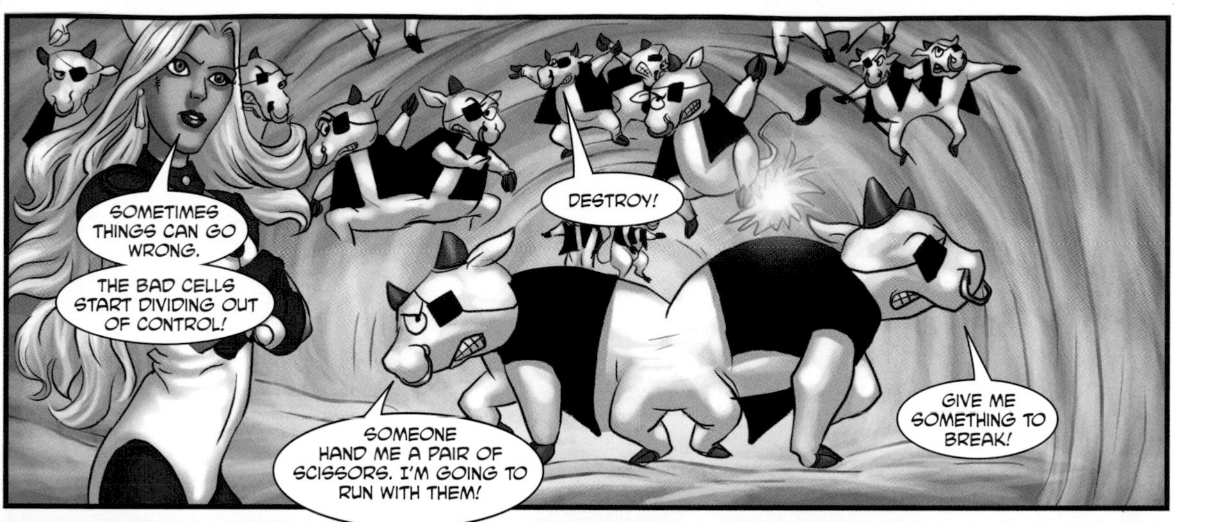
SOMETIMES THINGS CAN GO WRONG.
THE BAD CELLS START DIVIDING OUT OF CONTROL!
DESTROY!
SOMEONE HAND ME A PAIR OF SCISSORS. I'M GOING TO RUN WITH THEM!
GIVE ME SOMETHING TO BREAK!

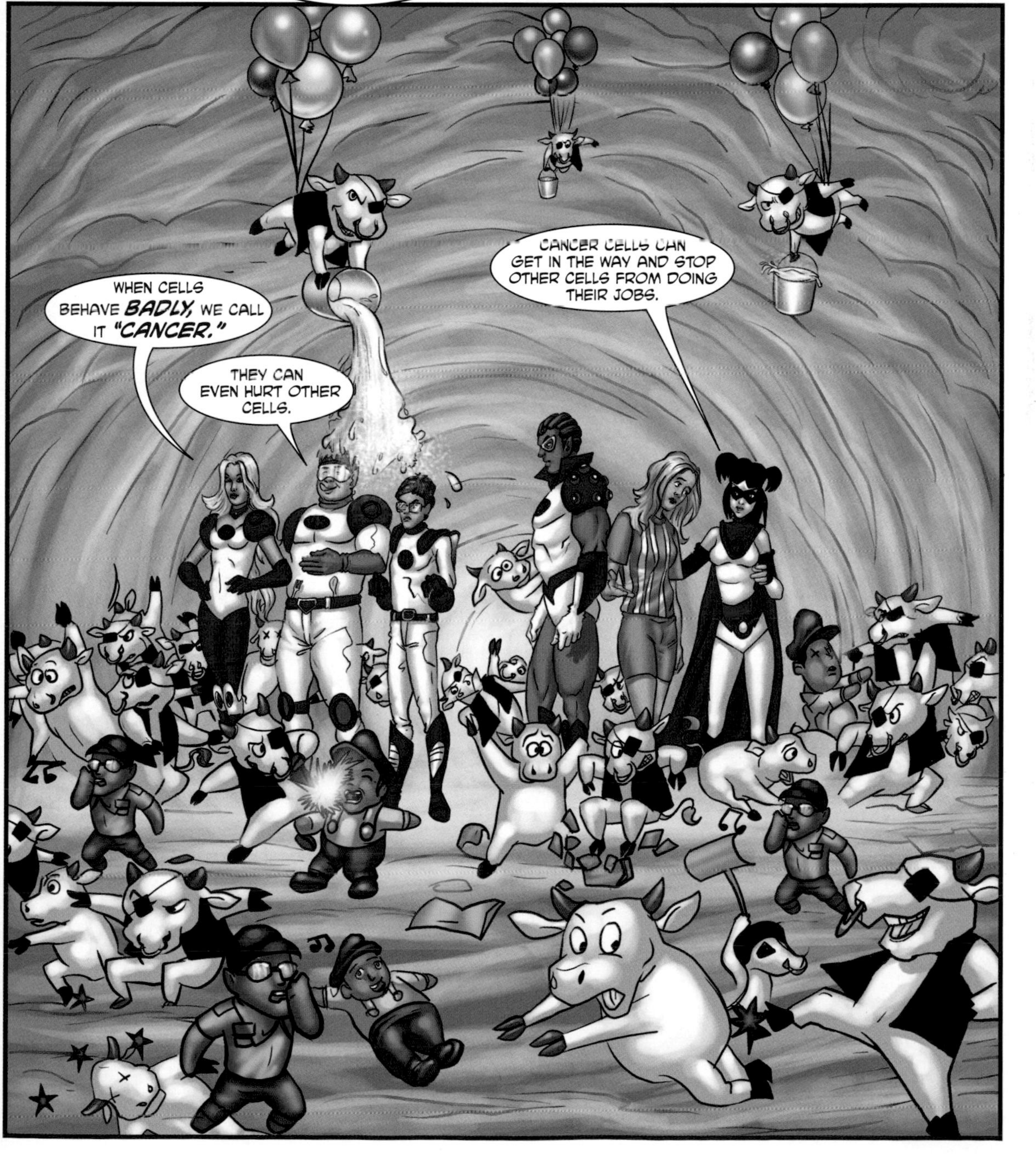
WHEN CELLS BEHAVE **BADLY,** WE CALL IT **"CANCER."**
THEY CAN EVEN HURT OTHER CELLS.
CANCER CELLS CAN GET IN THE WAY AND STOP OTHER CELLS FROM DOING THEIR JOBS.

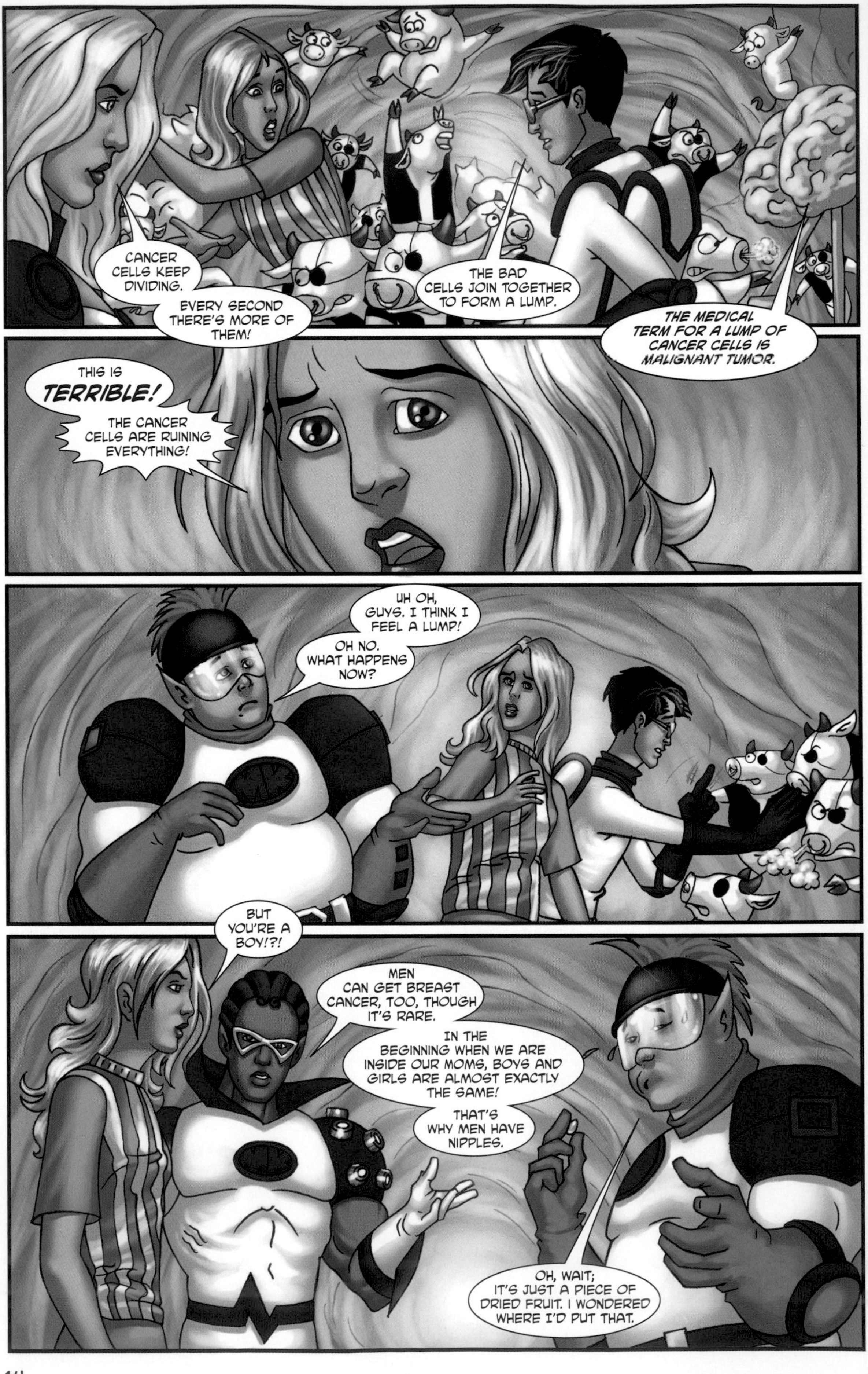
CANCER CELLS KEEP DIVIDING.
EVERY SECOND THERE'S MORE OF THEM!
THE BAD CELLS JOIN TOGETHER TO FORM A LUMP.
THE MEDICAL TERM FOR A LUMP OF CANCER CELLS IS MALIGNANT TUMOR.
THIS IS TERRIBLE!
THE CANCER CELLS ARE RUINING EVERYTHING!
UH OH, GUYS. I THINK I FEEL A LUMP!
OH NO. WHAT HAPPENS NOW?
BUT YOU'RE A BOY!?!
MEN CAN GET BREAST CANCER, TOO, THOUGH IT'S RARE.
IN THE BEGINNING WHEN WE ARE INSIDE OUR MOMS, BOYS AND GIRLS ARE ALMOST EXACTLY THE SAME!
THAT'S WHY MEN HAVE NIPPLES.
OH, WAIT; IT'S JUST A PIECE OF DRIED FRUIT. I WONDERED WHERE I'D PUT THAT.

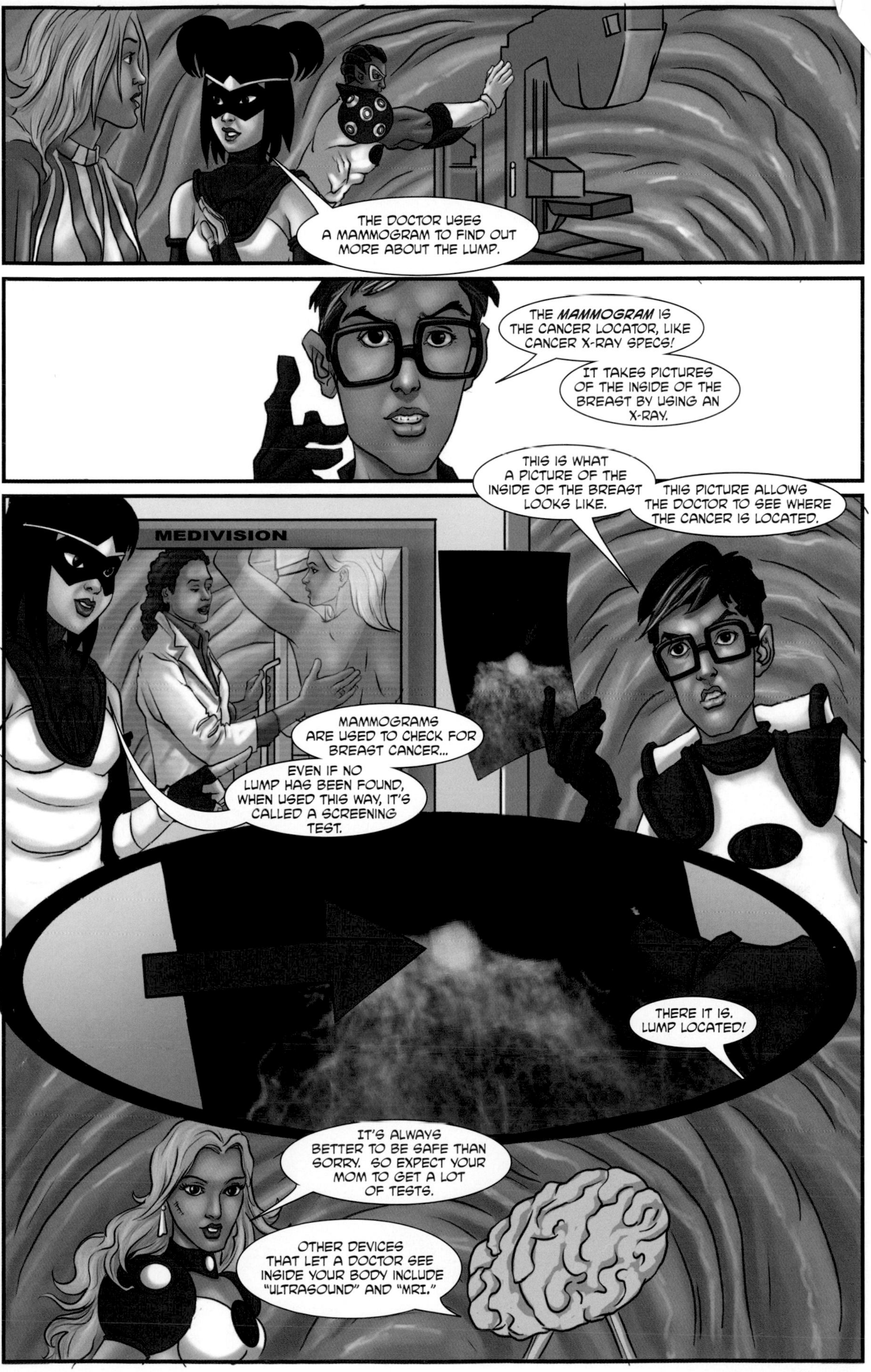
THE DOCTOR USES A MAMMOGRAM TO FIND OUT MORE ABOUT THE LUMP.
THE *MAMMOGRAM* IS THE CANCER LOCATOR, LIKE CANCER X-RAY SPECS!
IT TAKES PICTURES OF THE INSIDE OF THE BREAST BY USING AN X-RAY.
THIS IS WHAT A PICTURE OF THE INSIDE OF THE BREAST LOOKS LIKE.
THIS PICTURE ALLOWS THE DOCTOR TO SEE WHERE THE CANCER IS LOCATED.
MEDIVISION
MAMMOGRAMS ARE USED TO CHECK FOR BREAST CANCER...
EVEN IF NO LUMP HAS BEEN FOUND, WHEN USED THIS WAY, IT'S CALLED A SCREENING TEST.
THERE IT IS. LUMP LOCATED!
IT'S ALWAYS BETTER TO BE SAFE THAN SORRY. SO EXPECT YOUR MOM TO GET A LOT OF TESTS.
OTHER DEVICES THAT LET A DOCTOR SEE INSIDE YOUR BODY INCLUDE "ULTRASOUND" AND "MRI."

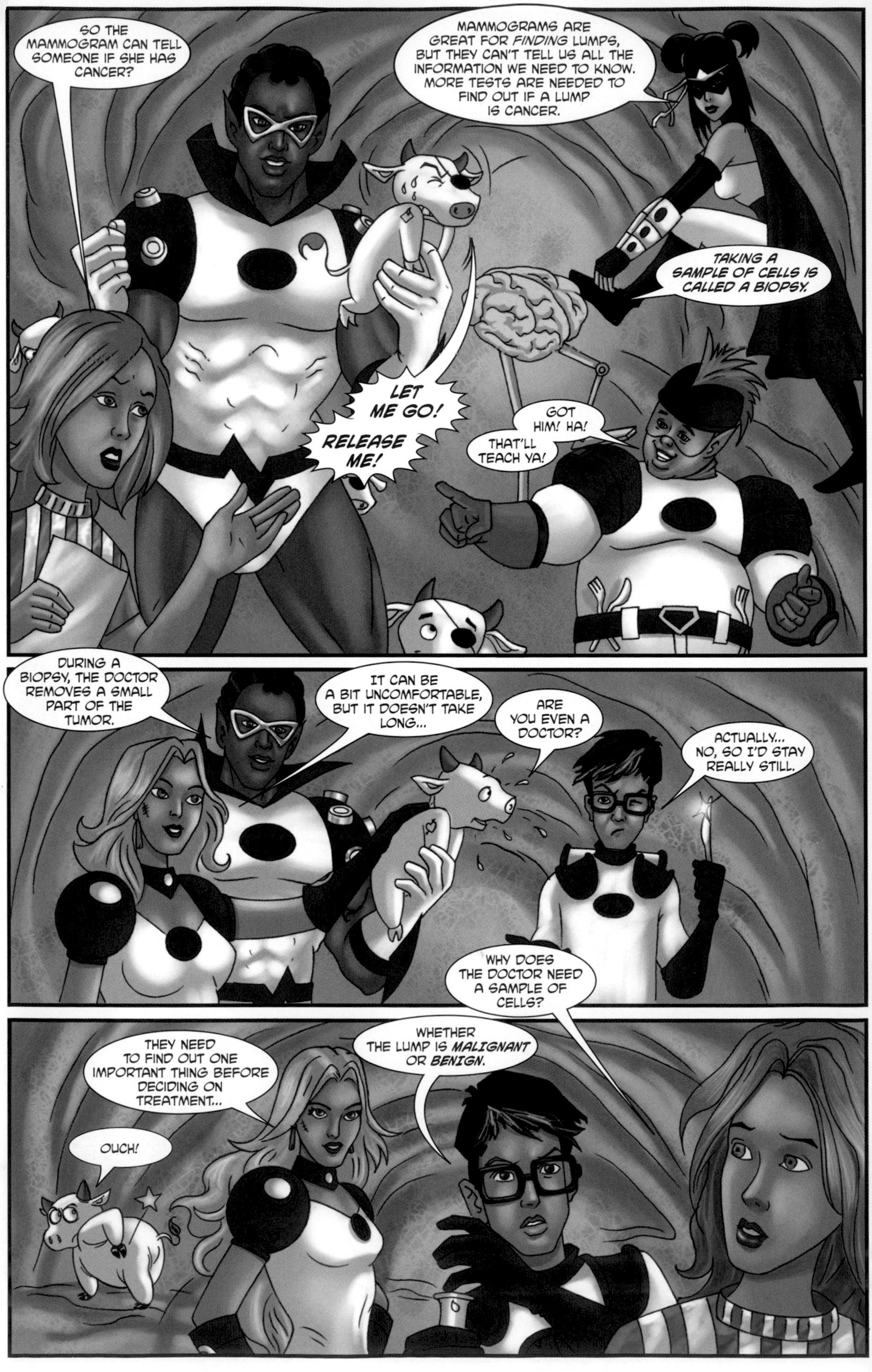
SO THE MAMMOGRAM CAN TELL SOMEONE IF SHE HAS CANCER?
MAMMOGRAMS ARE GREAT FOR *FINDING* LUMPS, BUT THEY CAN'T TELL US ALL THE INFORMATION WE NEED TO KNOW. MORE TESTS ARE NEEDED TO FIND OUT IF A LUMP IS CANCER.
TAKING A SAMPLE OF CELLS IS CALLED A BIOPSY.
LET ME GO!
RELEASE ME!
GOT HIM! HA!
THAT'LL TEACH YA!
DURING A BIOPSY, THE DOCTOR REMOVES A SMALL PART OF THE TUMOR.
IT CAN BE A BIT UNCOMFORTABLE, BUT IT DOESN'T TAKE LONG...
ARE YOU EVEN A DOCTOR?
ACTUALLY... NO, SO I'D STAY REALLY STILL.
WHY DOES THE DOCTOR NEED A SAMPLE OF CELLS?
THEY NEED TO FIND OUT ONE IMPORTANT THING BEFORE DECIDING ON TREATMENT...
WHETHER THE LUMP IS *MALIGNANT* OR *BENIGN*.
OUCH!

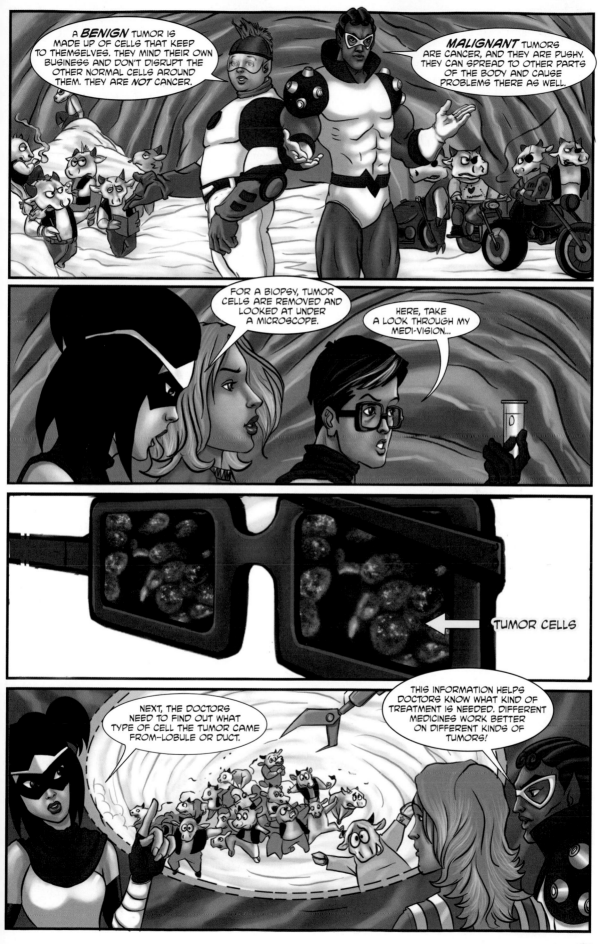

A *BENIGN* TUMOR IS MADE UP OF CELLS THAT KEEP TO THEMSELVES. THEY MIND THEIR OWN BUSINESS AND DON'T DISRUPT THE OTHER NORMAL CELLS AROUND THEM. THEY ARE *NOT* CANCER.

MALIGNANT TUMORS ARE CANCER, AND THEY ARE PUSHY. THEY CAN SPREAD TO OTHER PARTS OF THE BODY AND CAUSE PROBLEMS THERE AS WELL.

FOR A BIOPSY, TUMOR CELLS ARE REMOVED AND LOOKED AT UNDER A MICROSCOPE.

HERE, TAKE A LOOK THROUGH MY MEDI-VISION...

TUMOR CELLS

NEXT, THE DOCTORS NEED TO FIND OUT WHAT TYPE OF CELL THE TUMOR CAME FROM—LOBULE OR DUCT.

THIS INFORMATION HELPS DOCTORS KNOW WHAT KIND OF TREATMENT IS NEEDED. DIFFERENT MEDICINES WORK BETTER ON DIFFERENT KINDS OF TUMORS!

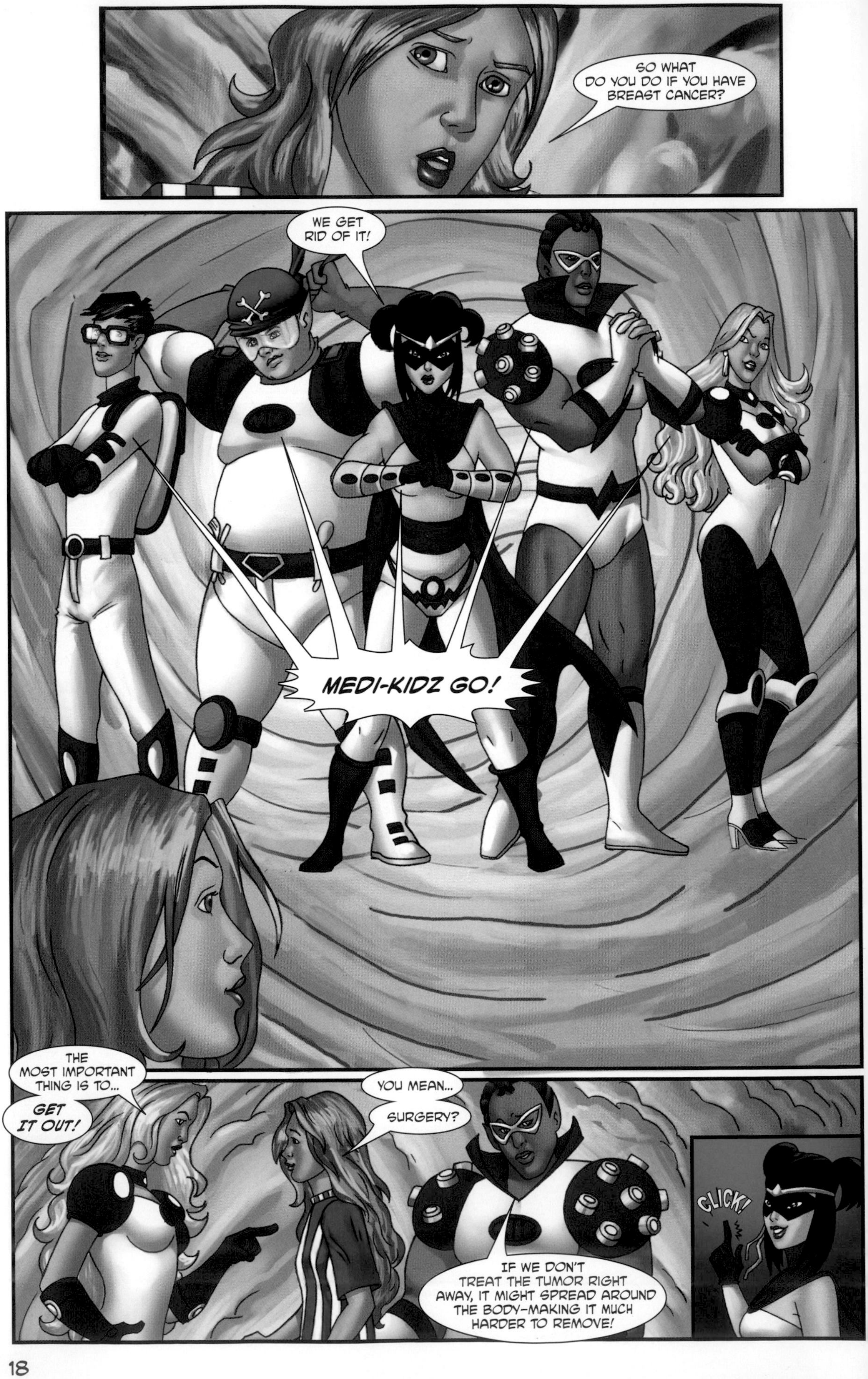
SO WHAT DO YOU DO IF YOU HAVE BREAST CANCER?
WE GET RID OF IT!
MEDI-KIDZ GO!
THE MOST IMPORTANT THING IS TO...
GET IT OUT!
YOU MEAN...
SURGERY?
IF WE DON'T TREAT THE TUMOR RIGHT AWAY, IT MIGHT SPREAD AROUND THE BODY–MAKING IT MUCH HARDER TO REMOVE!
CLICK!

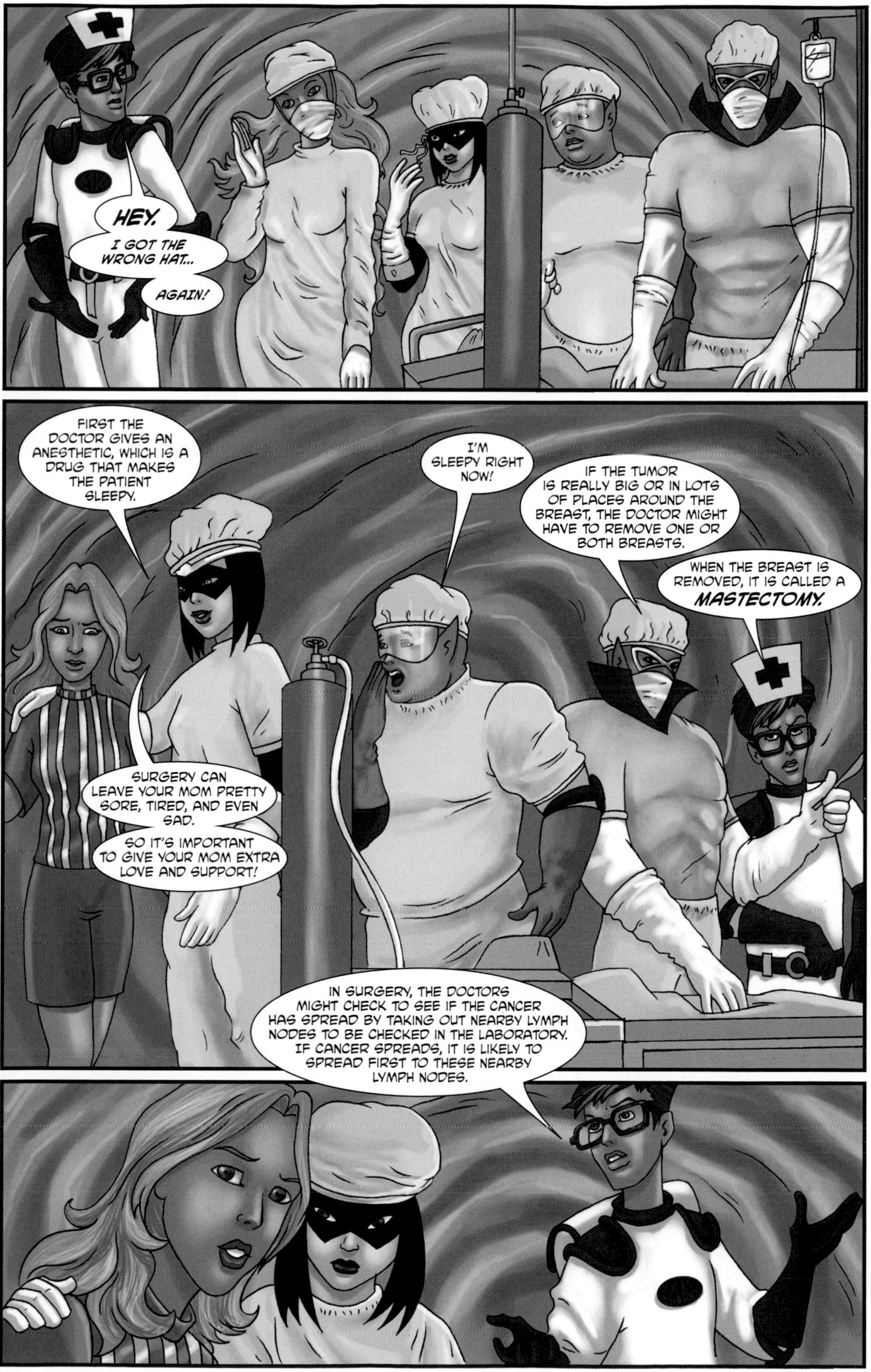
HEY.
I GOT THE WRONG HAT...
AGAIN!
FIRST THE DOCTOR GIVES AN ANESTHETIC, WHICH IS A DRUG THAT MAKES THE PATIENT SLEEPY.
I'M SLEEPY RIGHT NOW!
IF THE TUMOR IS REALLY BIG OR IN LOTS OF PLACES AROUND THE BREAST, THE DOCTOR MIGHT HAVE TO REMOVE ONE OR BOTH BREASTS.
WHEN THE BREAST IS REMOVED, IT IS CALLED A *MASTECTOMY.*
SURGERY CAN LEAVE YOUR MOM PRETTY SORE, TIRED, AND EVEN SAD.
SO IT'S IMPORTANT TO GIVE YOUR MOM EXTRA LOVE AND SUPPORT!
IN SURGERY, THE DOCTORS MIGHT CHECK TO SEE IF THE CANCER HAS SPREAD BY TAKING OUT NEARBY LYMPH NODES TO BE CHECKED IN THE LABORATORY. IF CANCER SPREADS, IT IS LIKELY TO SPREAD FIRST TO THESE NEARBY LYMPH NODES.

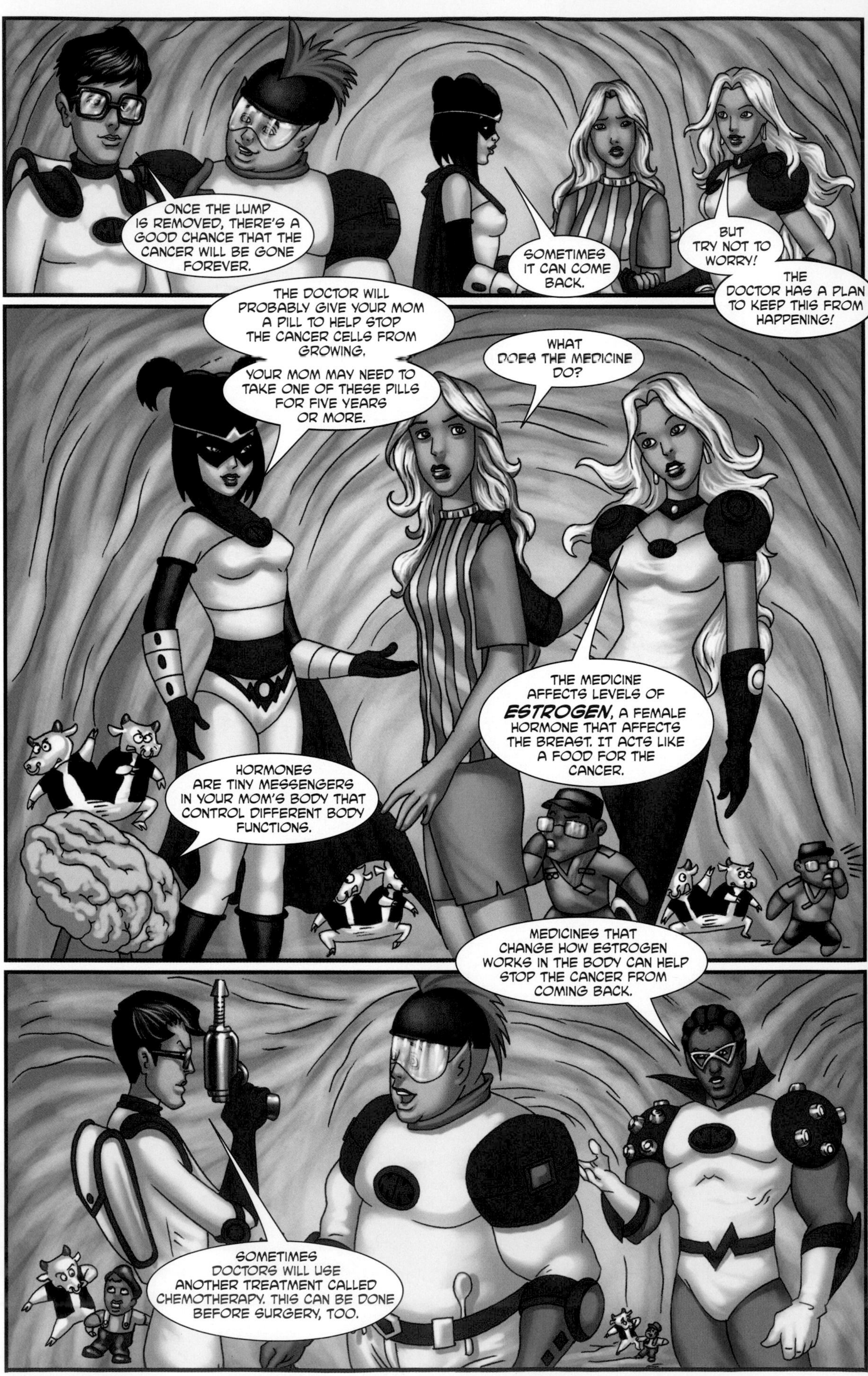

ONCE THE LUMP IS REMOVED, THERE'S A GOOD CHANCE THAT THE CANCER WILL BE GONE FOREVER.
SOMETIMES IT CAN COME BACK.
BUT TRY NOT TO WORRY!
THE DOCTOR HAS A PLAN TO KEEP THIS FROM HAPPENING!
THE DOCTOR WILL PROBABLY GIVE YOUR MOM A PILL TO HELP STOP THE CANCER CELLS FROM GROWING.
YOUR MOM MAY NEED TO TAKE ONE OF THESE PILLS FOR FIVE YEARS OR MORE.
WHAT DOES THE MEDICINE DO?
THE MEDICINE AFFECTS LEVELS OF ESTROGEN, A FEMALE HORMONE THAT AFFECTS THE BREAST. IT ACTS LIKE A FOOD FOR THE CANCER.
HORMONES ARE TINY MESSENGERS IN YOUR MOM'S BODY THAT CONTROL DIFFERENT BODY FUNCTIONS.
MEDICINES THAT CHANGE HOW ESTROGEN WORKS IN THE BODY CAN HELP STOP THE CANCER FROM COMING BACK.
SOMETIMES DOCTORS WILL USE ANOTHER TREATMENT CALLED CHEMOTHERAPY. THIS CAN BE DONE BEFORE SURGERY, TOO.

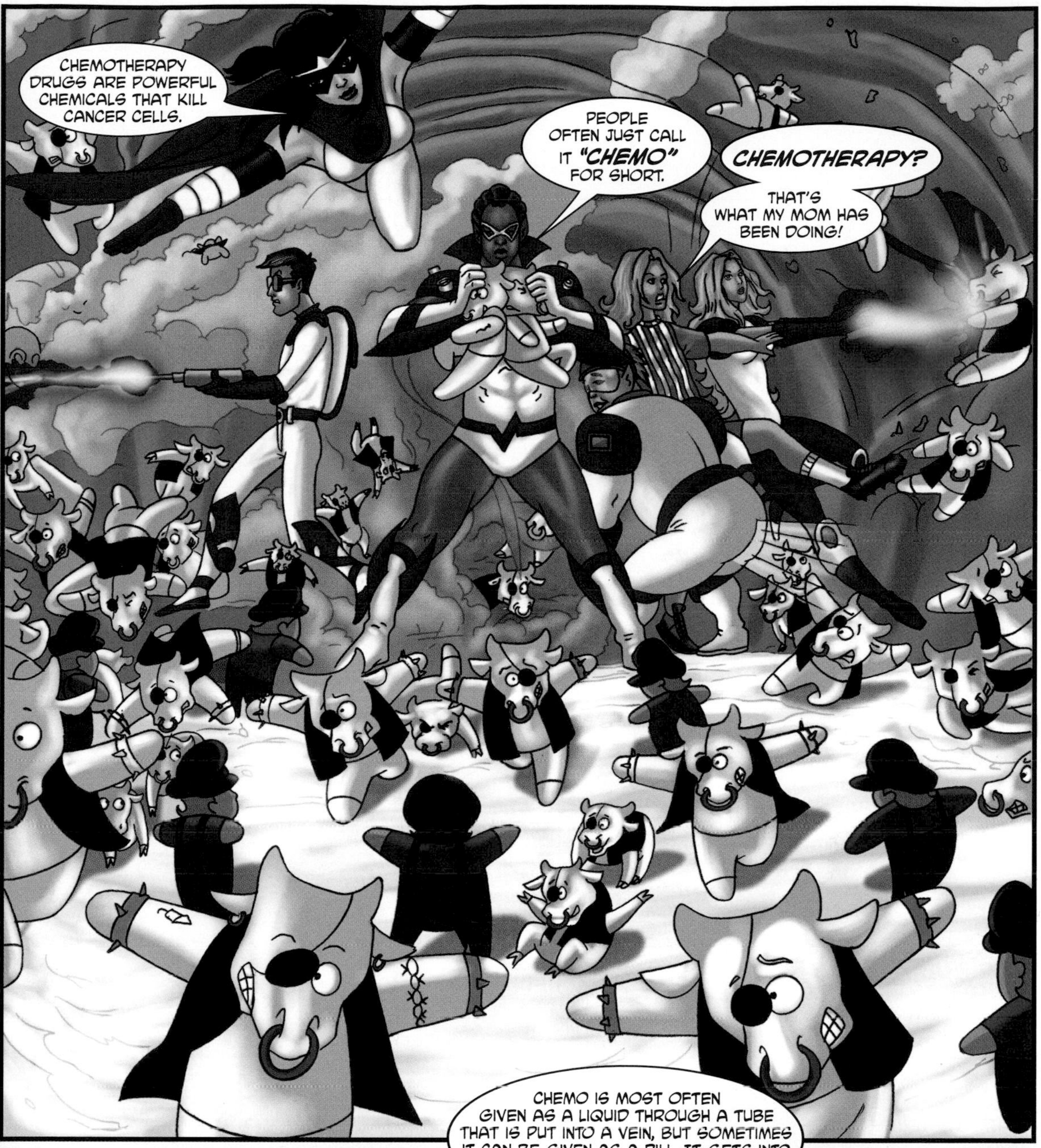
CHEMOTHERAPY DRUGS ARE POWERFUL CHEMICALS THAT KILL CANCER CELLS.
PEOPLE OFTEN JUST CALL IT "CHEMO" FOR SHORT.
CHEMOTHERAPY?
THAT'S WHAT MY MOM HAS BEEN DOING!

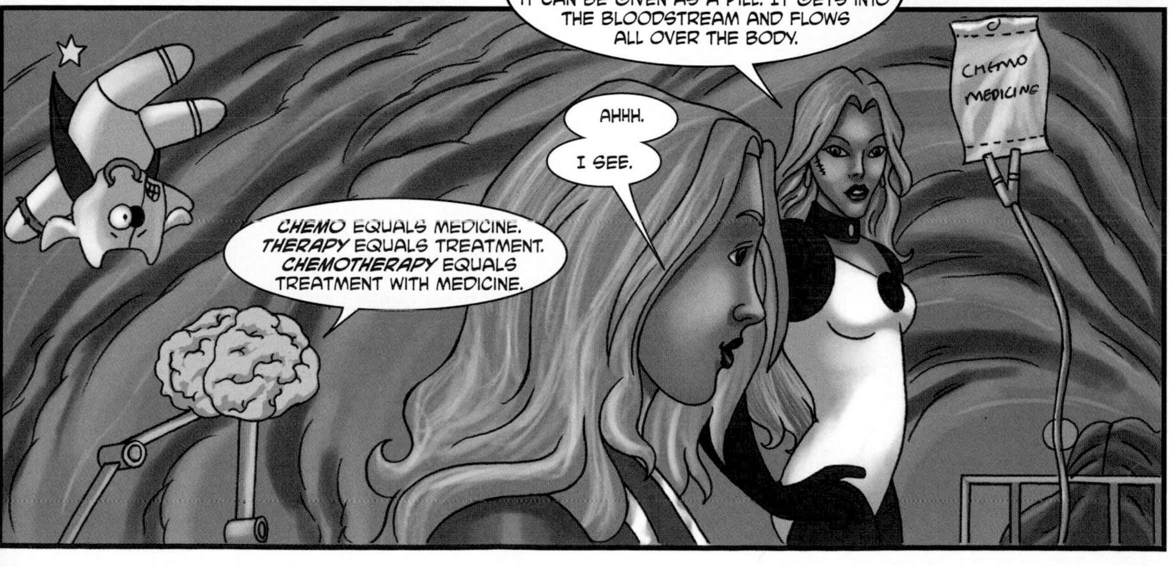
CHEMO IS MOST OFTEN GIVEN AS A LIQUID THROUGH A TUBE THAT IS PUT INTO A VEIN, BUT SOMETIMES IT CAN BE GIVEN AS A PILL. IT GETS INTO THE BLOODSTREAM AND FLOWS ALL OVER THE BODY.
CHEMO MEDICINE
AHHH.
I SEE.
CHEMO EQUALS MEDICINE. THERAPY EQUALS TREATMENT. CHEMOTHERAPY EQUALS TREATMENT WITH MEDICINE.

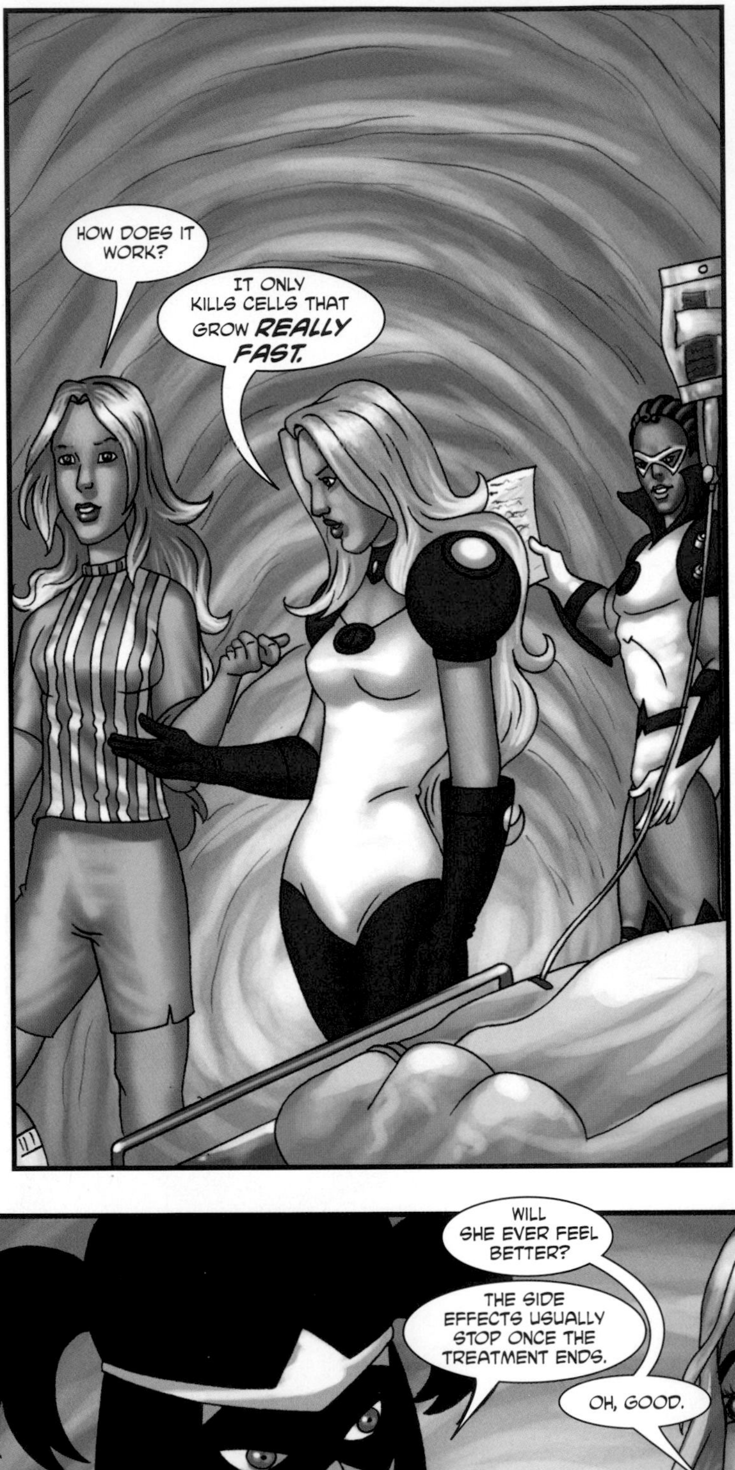
HOW DOES IT WORK?
IT ONLY KILLS CELLS THAT GROW REALLY FAST.

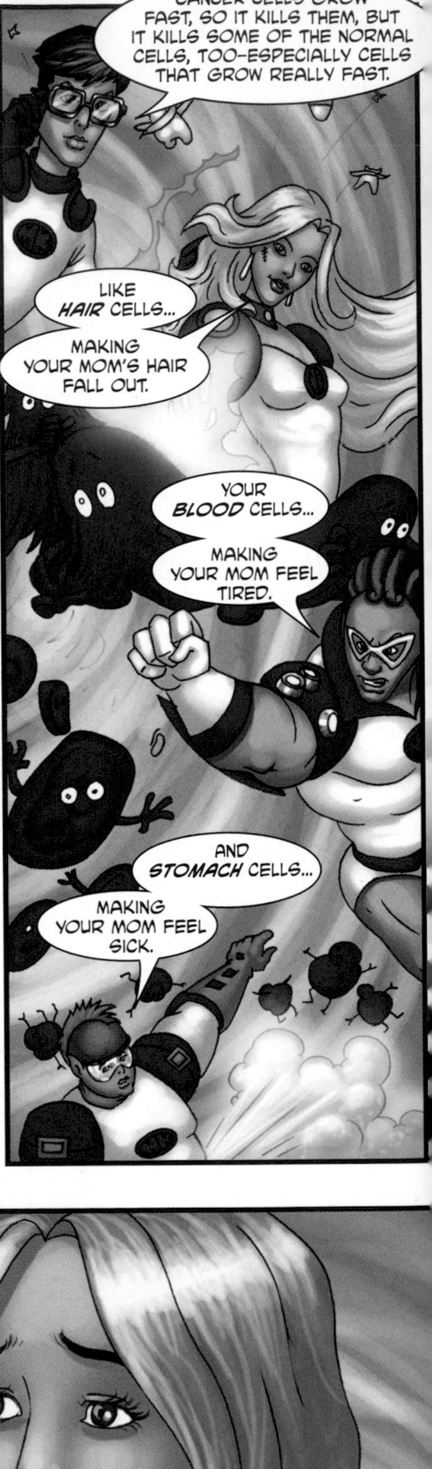
CANCER CELLS GROW FAST, SO IT KILLS THEM, BUT IT KILLS SOME OF THE NORMAL CELLS, TOO–ESPECIALLY CELLS THAT GROW REALLY FAST.
LIKE HAIR CELLS...
MAKING YOUR MOM'S HAIR FALL OUT.
YOUR BLOOD CELLS...
MAKING YOUR MOM FEEL TIRED.
AND STOMACH CELLS...
MAKING YOUR MOM FEEL SICK.

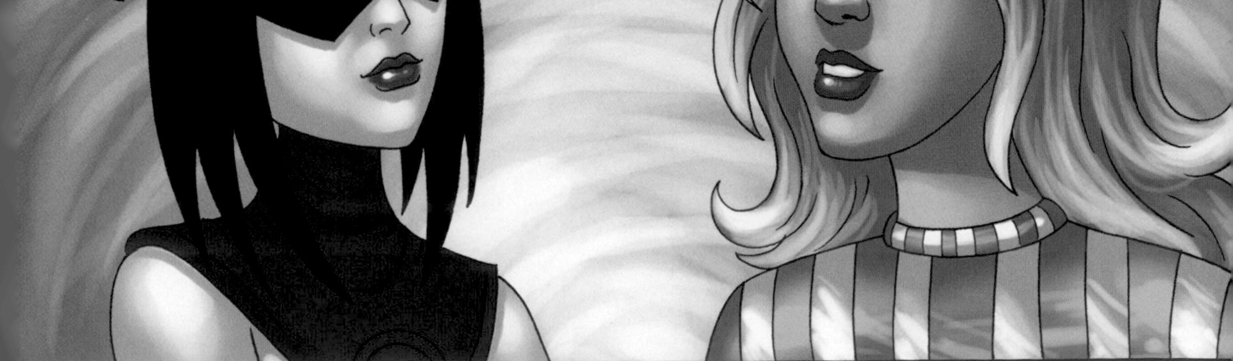
WILL SHE EVER FEEL BETTER?
THE SIDE EFFECTS USUALLY STOP ONCE THE TREATMENT ENDS.
OH, GOOD.

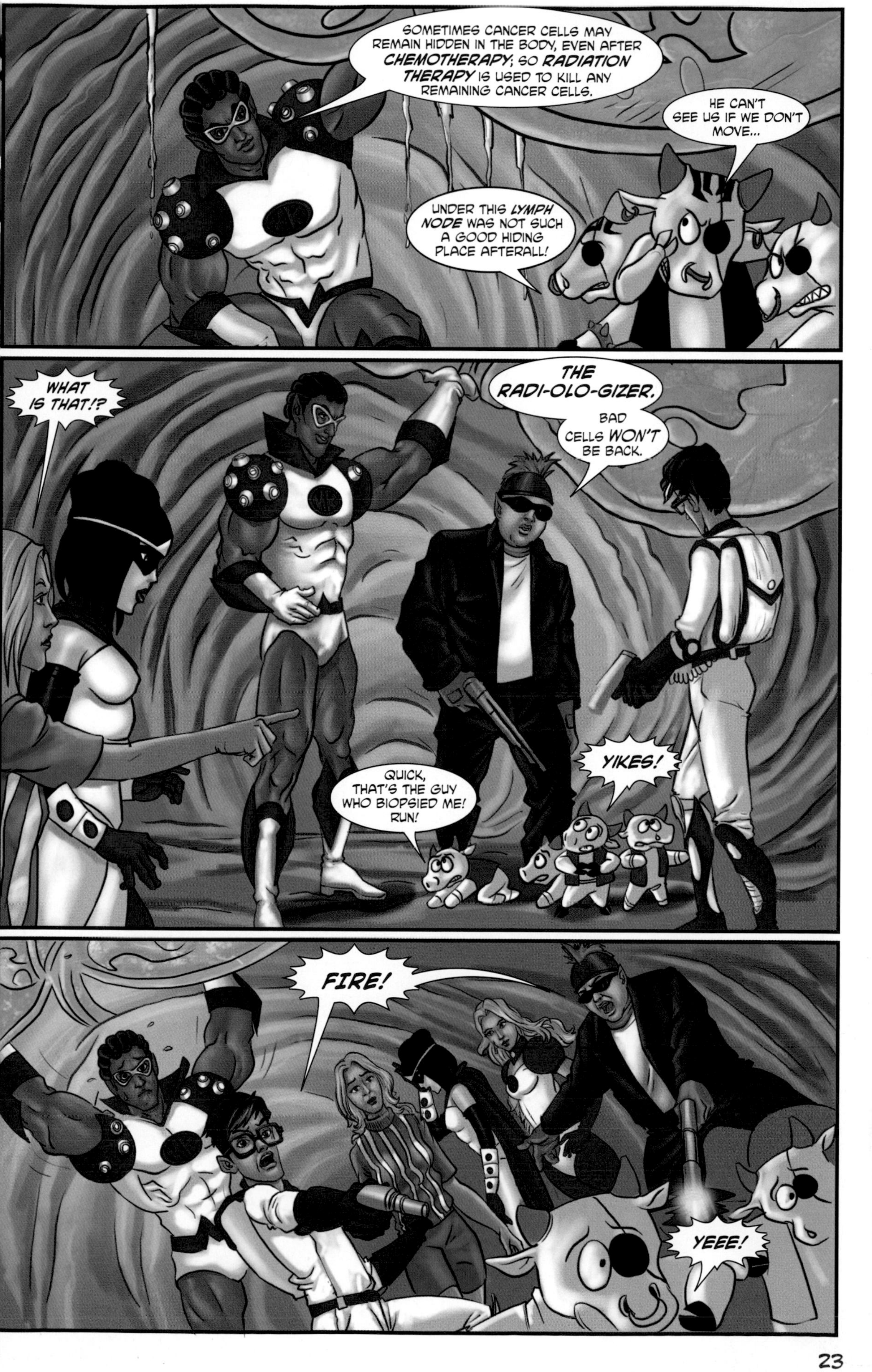
SOMETIMES CANCER CELLS MAY REMAIN HIDDEN IN THE BODY, EVEN AFTER CHEMOTHERAPY; SO RADIATION THERAPY IS USED TO KILL ANY REMAINING CANCER CELLS.
HE CAN'T SEE US IF WE DON'T MOVE...
UNDER THIS LYMPH NODE WAS NOT SUCH A GOOD HIDING PLACE AFTERALL!
WHAT IS THAT!?
THE RADI-OLO-GIZER.
BAD CELLS WON'T BE BACK.
QUICK, THAT'S THE GUY WHO BIOPSIED ME! RUN!
YIKES!
FIRE!
YEEE!

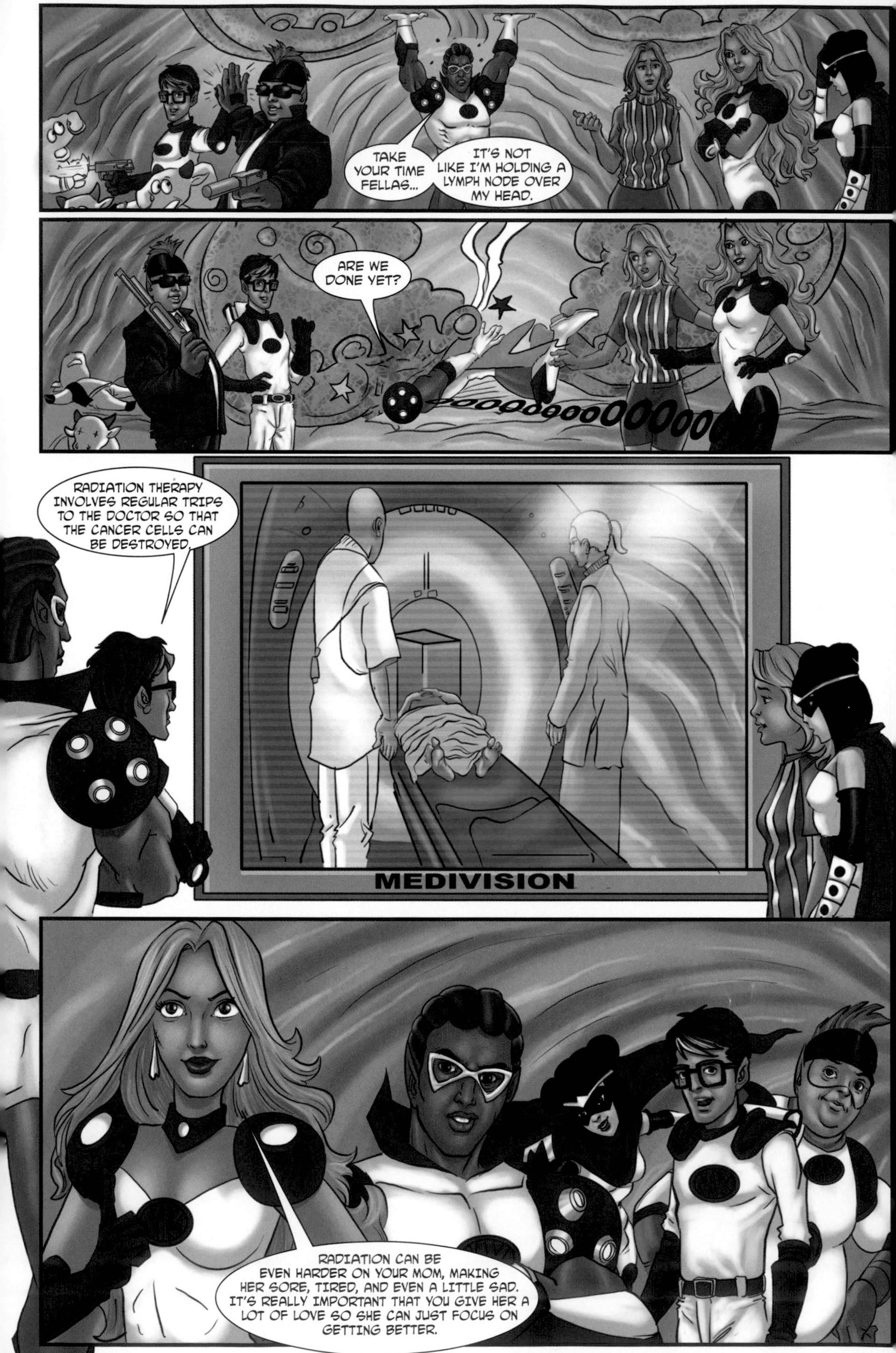

TAKE YOUR TIME FELLAS...
IT'S NOT LIKE I'M HOLDING A LYMPH NODE OVER MY HEAD.
ARE WE DONE YET?
RADIATION THERAPY INVOLVES REGULAR TRIPS TO THE DOCTOR SO THAT THE CANCER CELLS CAN BE DESTROYED.
MEDIVISION
RADIATION CAN BE EVEN HARDER ON YOUR MOM, MAKING HER SORE, TIRED, AND EVEN A LITTLE SAD. IT'S REALLY IMPORTANT THAT YOU GIVE HER A LOT OF LOVE SO SHE CAN JUST FOCUS ON GETTING BETTER.

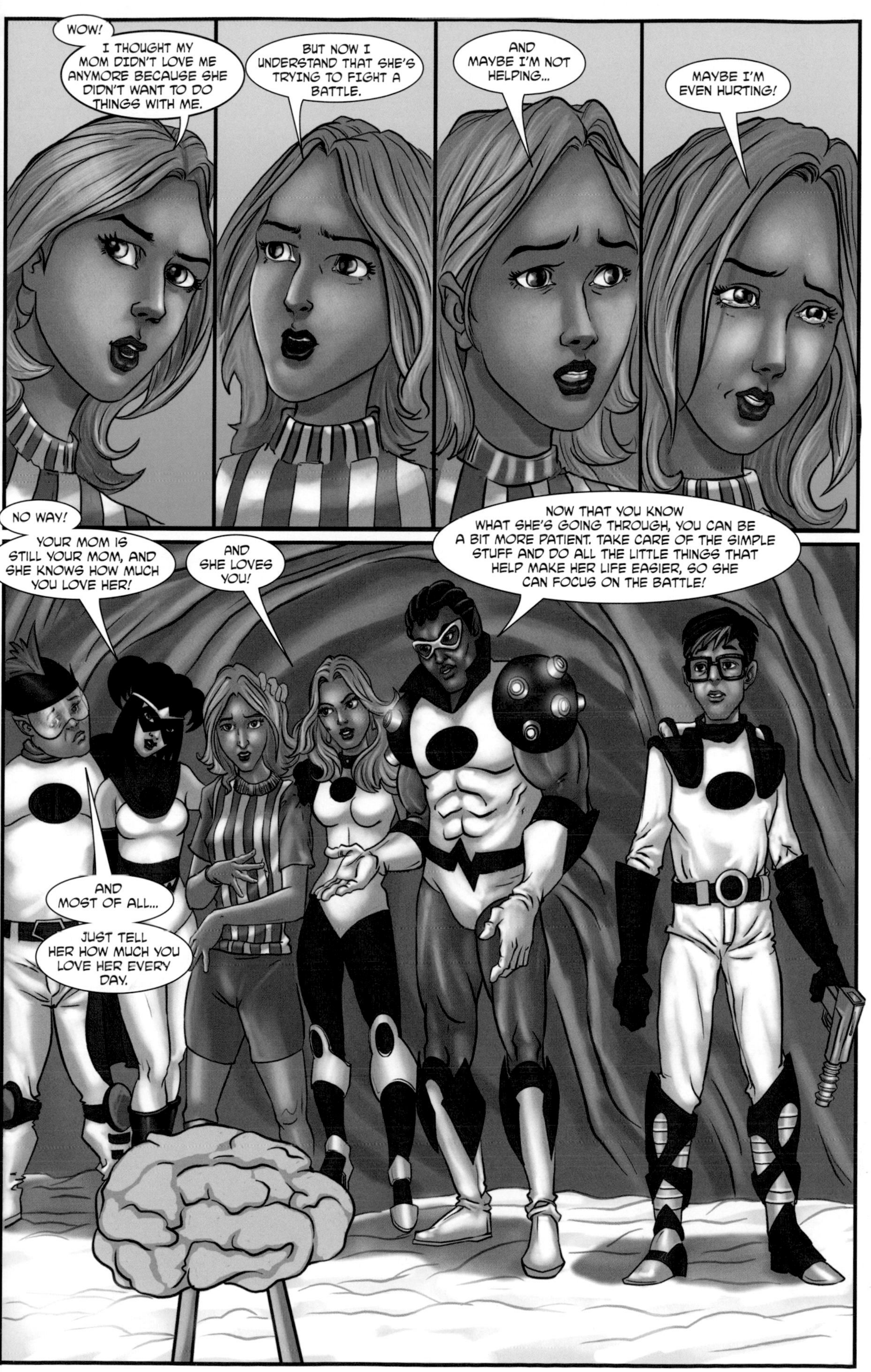
WOW!
I THOUGHT MY MOM DIDN'T LOVE ME ANYMORE BECAUSE SHE DIDN'T WANT TO DO THINGS WITH ME.
BUT NOW I UNDERSTAND THAT SHE'S TRYING TO FIGHT A BATTLE.
AND MAYBE I'M NOT HELPING...
MAYBE I'M EVEN HURTING!
NO WAY!
YOUR MOM IS STILL YOUR MOM, AND SHE KNOWS HOW MUCH YOU LOVE HER!
AND SHE LOVES YOU!
NOW THAT YOU KNOW WHAT SHE'S GOING THROUGH, YOU CAN BE A BIT MORE PATIENT. TAKE CARE OF THE SIMPLE STUFF AND DO ALL THE LITTLE THINGS THAT HELP MAKE HER LIFE EASIER, SO SHE CAN FOCUS ON THE BATTLE!
AND MOST OF ALL...
JUST TELL HER HOW MUCH YOU LOVE HER EVERY DAY.

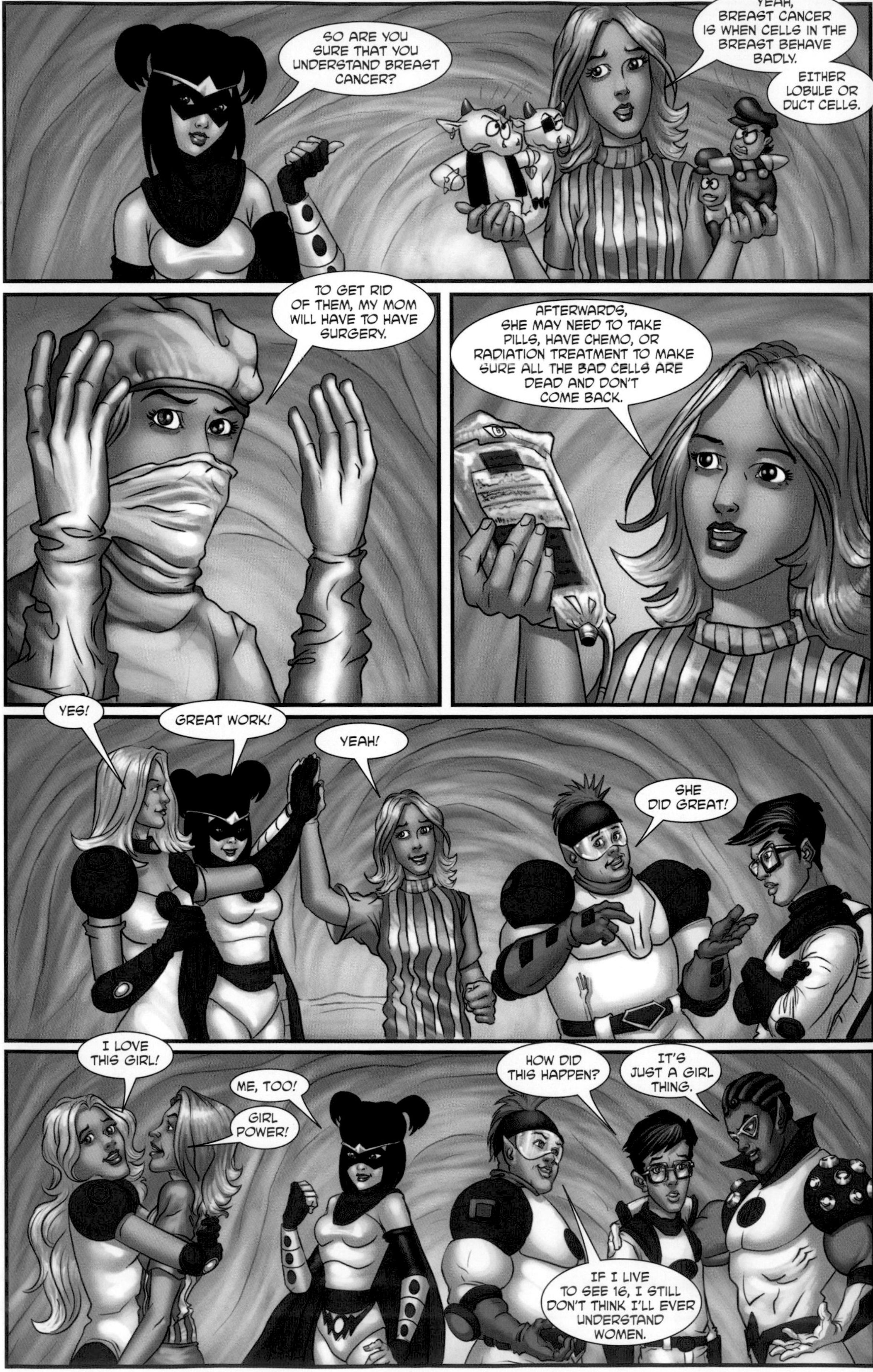
SO ARE YOU SURE THAT YOU UNDERSTAND BREAST CANCER?
YEAH, BREAST CANCER IS WHEN CELLS IN THE BREAST BEHAVE BADLY.
EITHER LOBULE OR DUCT CELLS.
TO GET RID OF THEM, MY MOM WILL HAVE TO HAVE SURGERY.
AFTERWARDS, SHE MAY NEED TO TAKE PILLS, HAVE CHEMO, OR RADIATION TREATMENT TO MAKE SURE ALL THE BAD CELLS ARE DEAD AND DON'T COME BACK.
YES!
GREAT WORK!
YEAH!
SHE DID GREAT!
I LOVE THIS GIRL!
ME, TOO!
GIRL POWER!
HOW DID THIS HAPPEN?
IT'S JUST A GIRL THING.
IF I LIVE TO SEE 16, I STILL DON'T THINK I'LL EVER UNDERSTAND WOMEN.

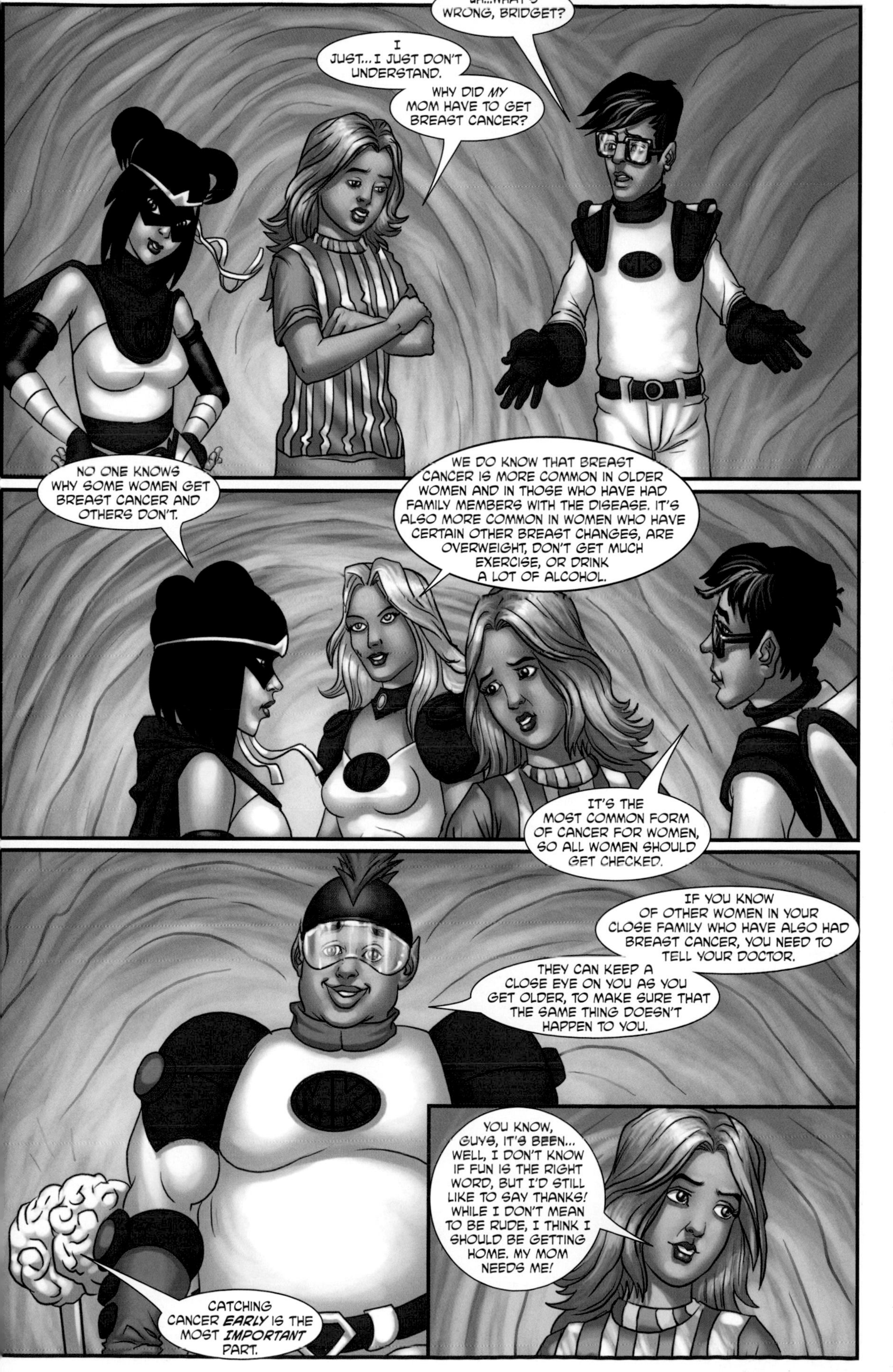
I JUST... I JUST DON'T UNDERSTAND.
UH...WHAT'S WRONG, BRIDGET?
WHY DID *MY* MOM HAVE TO GET BREAST CANCER?
NO ONE KNOWS WHY SOME WOMEN GET BREAST CANCER AND OTHERS DON'T.
WE DO KNOW THAT BREAST CANCER IS MORE COMMON IN OLDER WOMEN AND IN THOSE WHO HAVE HAD FAMILY MEMBERS WITH THE DISEASE. IT'S ALSO MORE COMMON IN WOMEN WHO HAVE CERTAIN OTHER BREAST CHANGES, ARE OVERWEIGHT, DON'T GET MUCH EXERCISE, OR DRINK A LOT OF ALCOHOL.
IT'S THE MOST COMMON FORM OF CANCER FOR WOMEN, SO ALL WOMEN SHOULD GET CHECKED.
IF YOU KNOW OF OTHER WOMEN IN YOUR CLOSE FAMILY WHO HAVE ALSO HAD BREAST CANCER, YOU NEED TO TELL YOUR DOCTOR.
THEY CAN KEEP A CLOSE EYE ON YOU AS YOU GET OLDER, TO MAKE SURE THAT THE SAME THING DOESN'T HAPPEN TO YOU.
CATCHING CANCER *EARLY* IS THE MOST *IMPORTANT* PART.
YOU KNOW, GUYS, IT'S BEEN... WELL, I DON'T KNOW IF FUN IS THE RIGHT WORD, BUT I'D STILL LIKE TO SAY THANKS! WHILE I DON'T MEAN TO BE RUDE, I THINK I SHOULD BE GETTING HOME. MY MOM NEEDS ME!

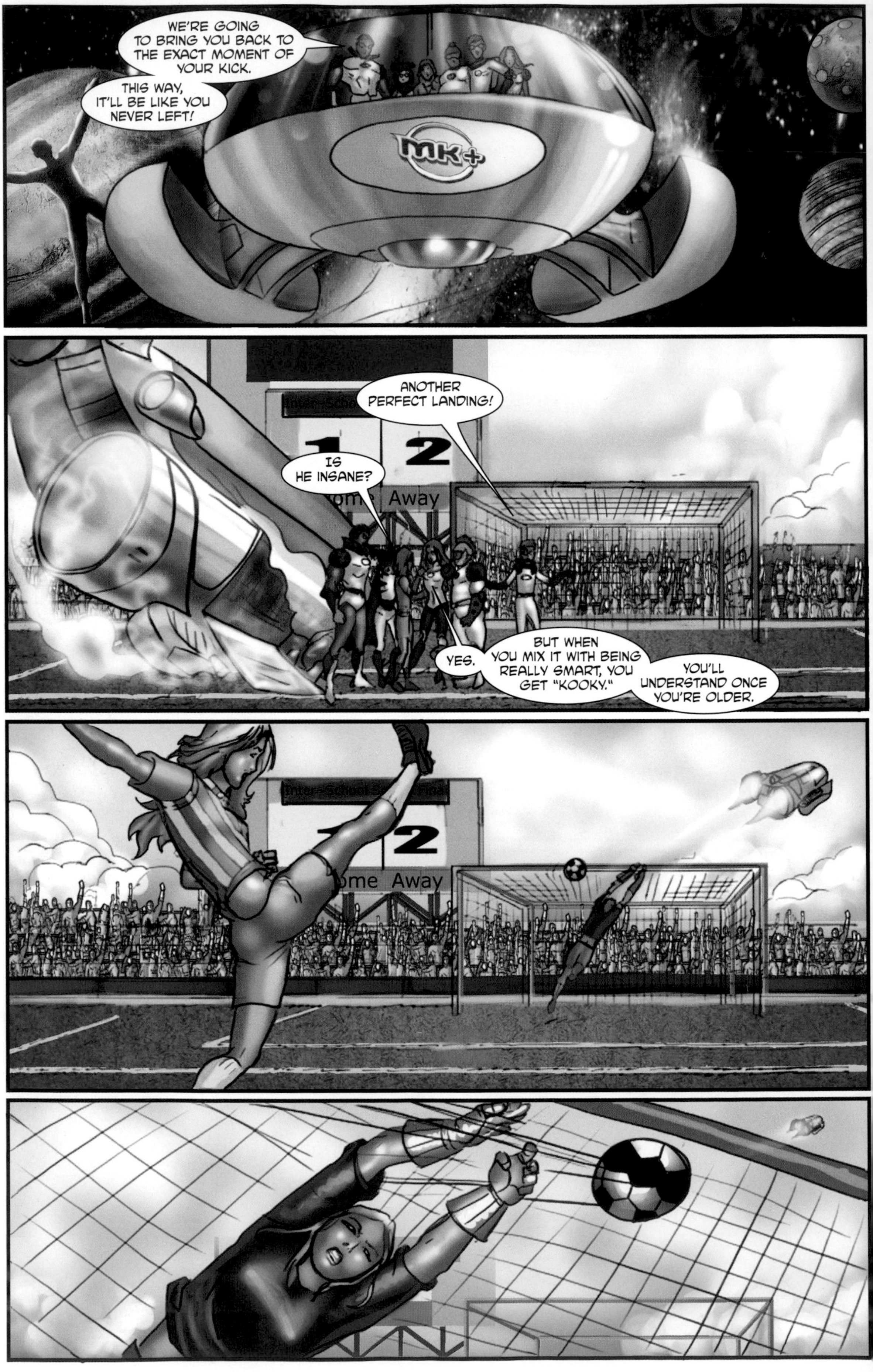
WE'RE GOING TO BRING YOU BACK TO THE EXACT MOMENT OF YOUR KICK.
THIS WAY, IT'LL BE LIKE YOU NEVER LEFT!
ANOTHER PERFECT LANDING!
IS HE INSANE?
YES.
BUT WHEN YOU MIX IT WITH BEING REALLY SMART, YOU GET "KOOKY."
YOU'LL UNDERSTAND ONCE YOU'RE OLDER.

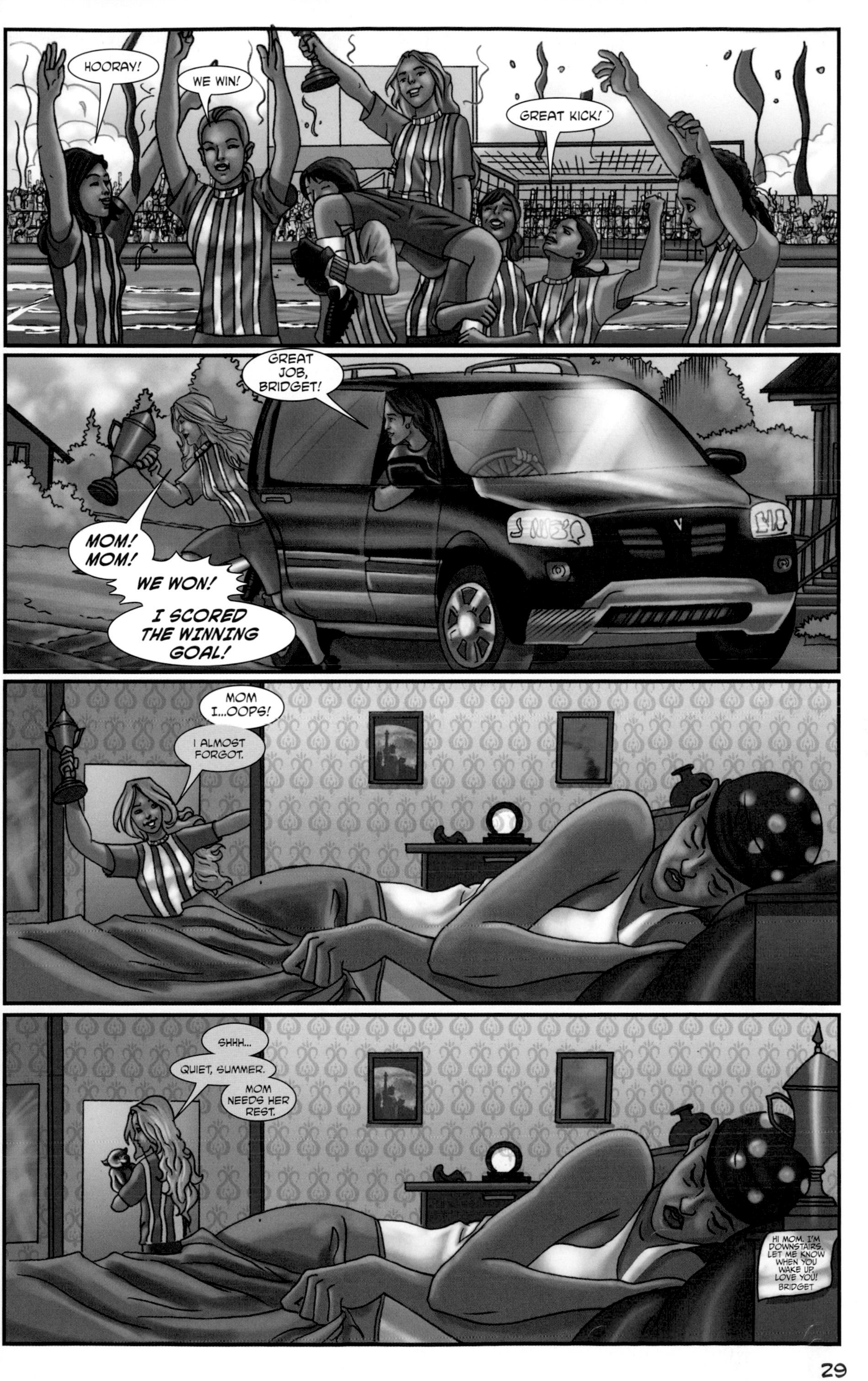
HOORAY!
WE WIN!
GREAT KICK!
GREAT JOB, BRIDGET!
MOM! MOM!
WE WON!
I SCORED THE WINNING GOAL!
MOM I...OOPS!
I ALMOST FORGOT.
SHHH...
QUIET, SUMMER.
MOM NEEDS HER REST.
HI MOM. I'M DOWNSTAIRS. LET ME KNOW WHEN YOU WAKE UP. LOVE YOU! BRIDGET

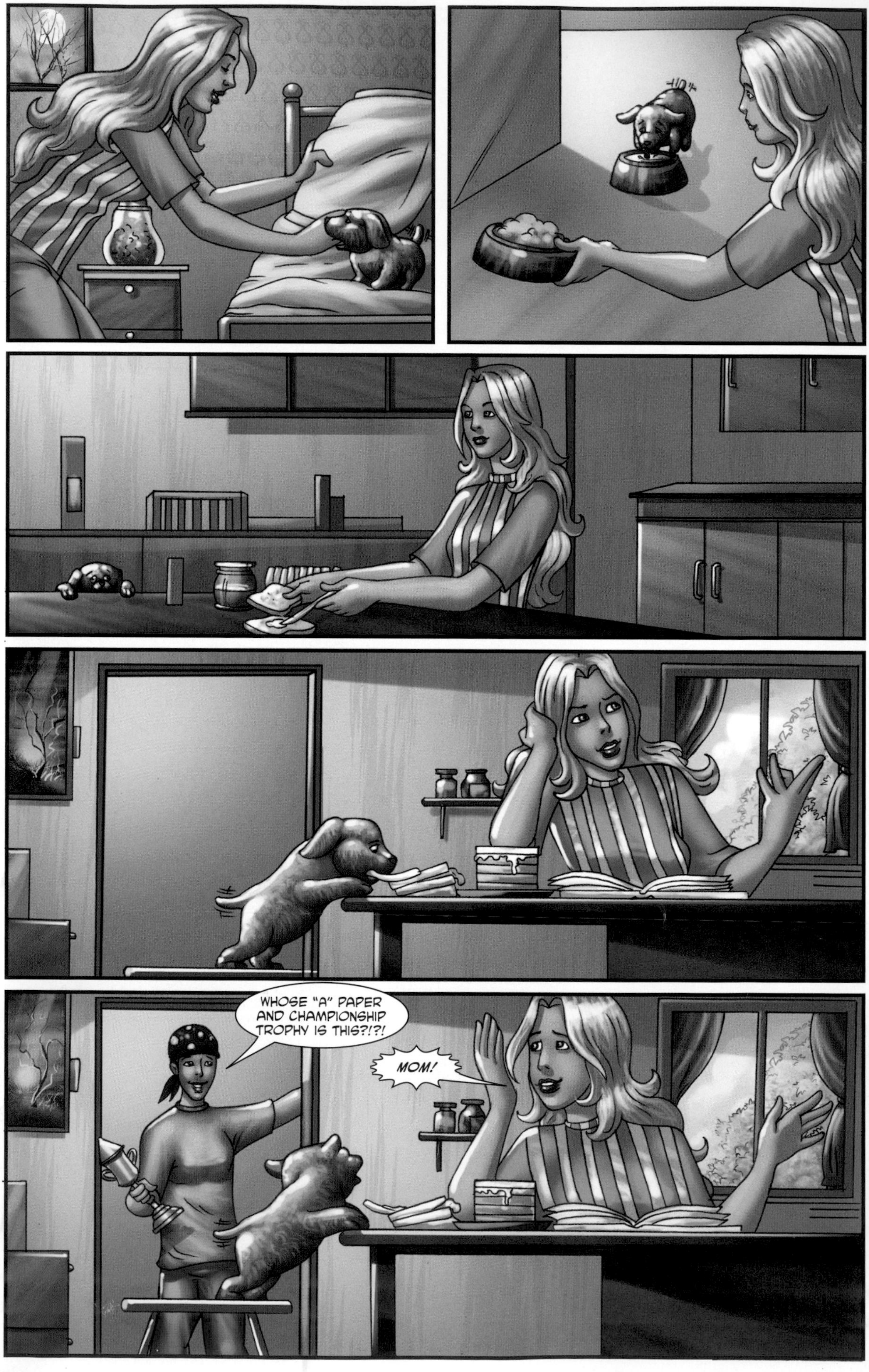

WHOSE "A" PAPER AND CHAMPIONSHIP TROPHY IS THIS?!?!
MOM!

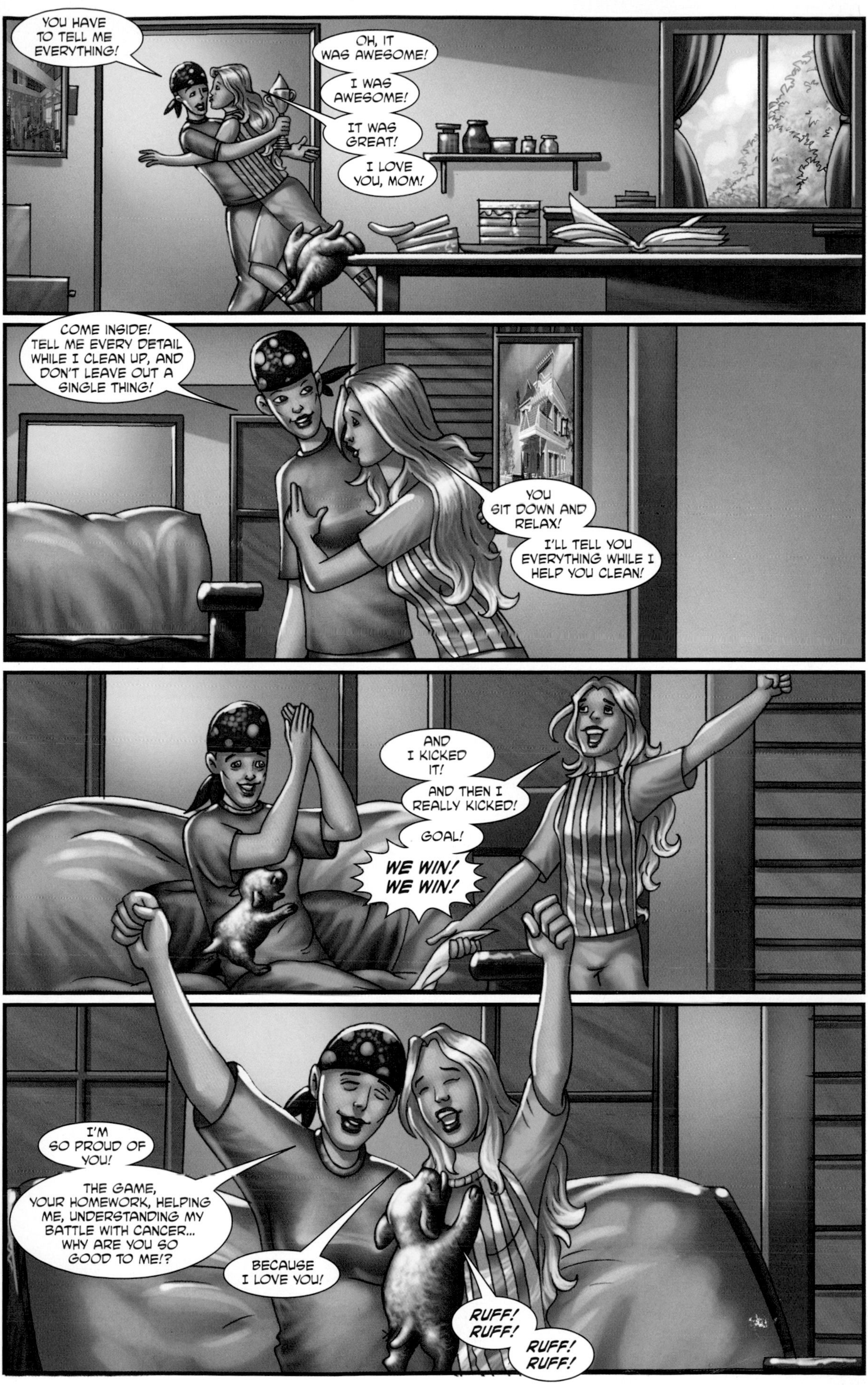

YOU HAVE TO TELL ME EVERYTHING!
OH, IT WAS AWESOME!
I WAS AWESOME!
IT WAS GREAT!
I LOVE YOU, MOM!
COME INSIDE! TELL ME EVERY DETAIL WHILE I CLEAN UP, AND DON'T LEAVE OUT A SINGLE THING!
YOU SIT DOWN AND RELAX!
I'LL TELL YOU EVERYTHING WHILE I HELP YOU CLEAN!
AND I KICKED IT!
AND THEN I REALLY KICKED!
GOAL!
WE WIN! WE WIN!
I'M SO PROUD OF YOU!
THE GAME, YOUR HOMEWORK, HELPING ME, UNDERSTANDING MY BATTLE WITH CANCER... WHY ARE YOU SO GOOD TO ME!?
BECAUSE I LOVE YOU!
RUFF! RUFF!
RUFF! RUFF!

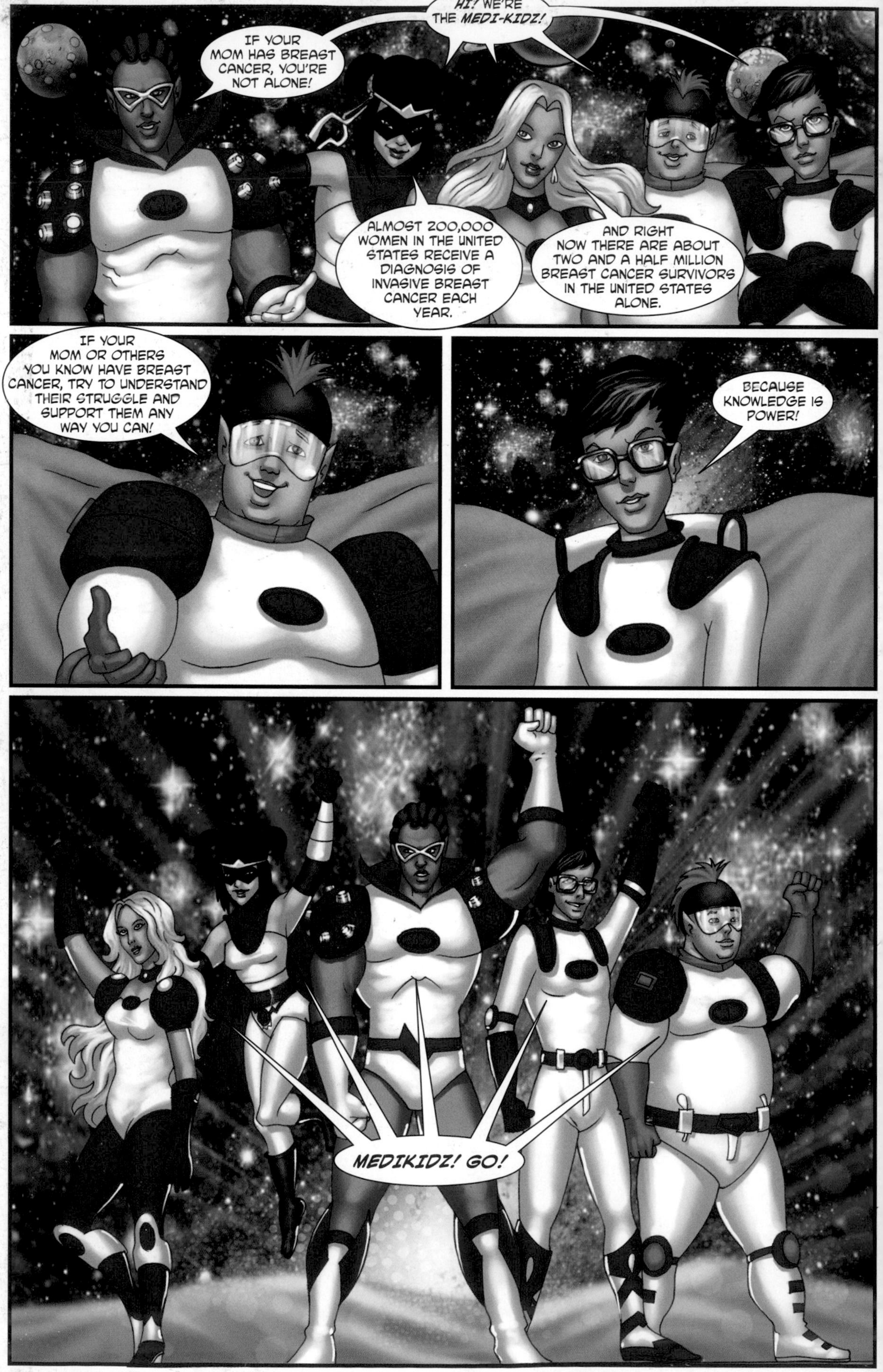
IF YOUR MOM HAS BREAST CANCER, YOU'RE NOT ALONE!
HI! WE'RE THE MEDI-KIDZ!
ALMOST 200,000 WOMEN IN THE UNITED STATES RECEIVE A DIAGNOSIS OF INVASIVE BREAST CANCER EACH YEAR.
AND RIGHT NOW THERE ARE ABOUT TWO AND A HALF MILLION BREAST CANCER SURVIVORS IN THE UNITED STATES ALONE.
IF YOUR MOM OR OTHERS YOU KNOW HAVE BREAST CANCER, TRY TO UNDERSTAND THEIR STRUGGLE AND SUPPORT THEM ANY WAY YOU CAN!
BECAUSE KNOWLEDGE IS POWER!
MEDIKIDZ! GO!